"I think you better kiss me," Audrey said.

"What?" Had he heard correctly? "You want me to kiss you?"

"Yes."

"Why?"

"I think that would be obvious."

Vincenzo was not used to people implying he was thick. "Explain it to me."

"Because if we don't have the chemistry to make it through a single kiss, the rest of this interview is an exercise in futility. Since you're so set on us being physically compatible."

It actually made sense and he had not considered it, because he'd been so intent on *not* giving in to his urge to kiss her.

He nodded and stood up, away from the desk, putting his hand out to her. "That is an excellent point."

Curling his fingers around her hand, he pulled her to her feet, her body coming within inches of his own.

Their gazes locked, hers filled with trepidation and something else that he had been unsure he would find there: desire.

"You want me."

"I want a kiss," she corrected, but the truth was there.

Dear Reader,

Growing up, no matter how harsh life had gotten, my mom always made Christmas magical for us. I have very few good memories related to my dad, but Christmas mornings are one of them. From the big sooty boot prints he made from our fireplace to the Christmas tree to convince us Santa had come, to the cradle and high chair he made for my baby doll when I was seven, it was the one time a year I could remember him being a real dad.

My mom insisted Christmas miracles happened, and every year he managed to be a dad for that one day, I knew she was right. By the time I was ten, my dad was no longer around on Christmas, or any other day, but the certainty in the magic of the holidays never left me.

My husband and I have tried to give magical moments to our own children and those we've taken in over the years. And while Tom is an amazing dad every day of the year, I have to say he outshines himself at Christmas, too.

Hoping with my whole heart that you experience a little holiday magic this year!

Much love,

Lucy

Lucy Monroe

—

Million Dollar Christmas Proposal

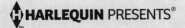

HARLEQUIN PRESENTS®

Recycling programs
for this product may
not exist in your area.

ISBN-13: 978-0-373-13191-4

MILLION DOLLAR CHRISTMAS PROPOSAL

Copyright © 2013 by Lucy Monroe

HARLEQUIN®

Printed in U.S.A.

™ www.Harlequin.com

All about the author...
Lucy Monroe

Award-winning and bestselling author **LUCY MONROE** sold her first book in September of 2002 to Harlequin Presents®. That book represented a dream that had been burning in her heart for years...the dream to share her stories with readers who love romance as much as she does. Since then she has sold more than thirty books to three publishers and hit national bestseller lists in the United States and England, but what has touched her most deeply since selling that first book are the reader letters she receives. Her most important goal with every book is to touch a reader's heart, and when she hears she's done that, it makes every night spent writing into the wee hours of the morning worth it.

She started reading Harlequin Presents® novels at a very young age and discovered a heroic type of man between the covers of those books...an honorable man, capable of faithfulness and sacrifice for the people he loves. Now married to what she terms her "alpha male at the end of a book," Lucy believes there is a lot more reality to the fantasy stories she writes than most people give credit for. She believes in happy endings that are really marvelous beginnings and that's why she writes them. She hopes her books help readers to believe a little, too...just like romance did for her so many years ago.

She really does love to hear from readers and responds to every email. You can reach her by emailing lucymonroe@lucymonroe.com.

Other titles by Lucy Monroe available in ebook format:

PRINCE OF SECRETS *(By His Royal Decree)*
ONE NIGHT HEIR *(By His Royal Decree)*
NOT JUST THE GREEK'S WIFE
HEART OF A DESERT WARRIOR

For my niece Hannah, because you are a big part of my holiday magic. Thank you for helping me and Isabelle decorate for Christmas and especially for your patience and creativity in decorating my "Mr. Monk" color-coordinated, every ornament evenly spaced tree each year. Few teenagers would be nearly so accepting of my OCD tendencies. Your parents raised you right and I'm in awe of what a lovely and strong young woman you truly are. Love you!

And with a special hug for all the teens that find themselves scrambling for a place to sleep this holiday season. It is my sincerest hope you find warmth and safety wrapped in holiday joy. That as my husband and I have opened our home to some, so might others open theirs to you. Blessings and love!

PROLOGUE

Eyes dry, heart shattered, Audrey Miller sat in the chair beside her baby brother's hospital bed and prayed for him to wake up.

He'd been in a coma since the ambulance brought him in three days ago and she wasn't leaving him. *She wasn't letting go of him.* Not like their parents had done.

Not like their two older siblings had.

How could family act like strangers? Worse than strangers? The rest of the Miller clan had cruelly rejected the incredibly sweet, scary-smart twelve-year-old boy. All because he'd told their parents he was gay.

He was *twelve,* for heaven's sake. What difference did it make?

But when he'd refused to recant his words, had insisted it wasn't some kind of phase or confusion despite his tender years, their parents had kicked him out.

Audrey couldn't even imagine it. She wouldn't have known what do at that age, alone and homeless. Toby had, though.

With nothing more than his saved-up allowance, his laptop, and a backpack full of clothes, he'd made his way south the two hundred miles from Boston to New York.

He hadn't called ahead, hadn't questioned. He'd just come to Audrey. He'd trusted her to be there for him when the rest of the family wasn't and she would never betray that trust.

Audrey hadn't thought it could get any worse than her parents kicking Toby out, had been sure that given time to consider their actions they would change their minds and let him move back home. They lived in one of the most progressive cities in the country, for goodness' sake.

But Carol and Randall Miller were not progressive people. She just hadn't realized how very steeped in narrow-minded conservatism they were.

Not until they gave her an ultimatum: remain a member in good standing with the rest of the family or stick by Toby. They'd made it clear that if she stuck by her little brother and supported him in any way they would withdraw all financial support and cut off all contact with Audrey.

Their plan to scare both of their youngest children into compliance with their strict viewpoint of the world had backfired.

Audrey had refused and when Toby had learned what that cost her, he'd tried to kill himself. Toby had used the Swiss Army knife their father had given him for his twelfth birthday to cut his wrists.

It hadn't been a cry for help; it had been a testament to his utter wretchedness at their parents' total rejection. He did it when the house she shared with three other Barnard students was supposed to be empty for several hours.

If Audrey's roommate hadn't forgotten a paper she had to turn in and gone back to the house, if Liz hadn't investigated the running shower when Toby hadn't answered her call, he would have died there, his blood washing down the drain of their old-fashioned porcelain tub.

"I love you, Toby. You have to come back to me. You're a good person." And she would tell him that as many times as it took. "Come back. Please, Toby. I love you."

Toby's eyelids fluttered and then a dazed brown gaze met hers. "Audrey?"

"Yes. Sweetheart. I'm here."

"I…" He looked confused.

She leaned over the bed and kissed his forehead. "You listen to me, Tobias Daniel Miller. You are my family. The only one that counts. Don't you ever try to leave me again."

"If I wasn't here you'd be okay with Mom and Dad."

"I'd rather have you," she promised.

"No, I—"

"Stop. I mean it, Tobe. You're my brother and I love you. You know how much it hurts that Mom and Dad don't love us because we aren't exactly what they want us to be?"

His mouth twisted with pain, his dark eyes haunted. "Yes."

"Times that by a million and then you'll know how much I'd hurt if I lost you. Okay?"

Then she saw something in her little brother's eyes that she would do anything to keep there. A spark of hope amidst the desolation.

"Okay."

It was a promise. Toby wouldn't give up on himself again and neither would Audrey. Not ever.

CHAPTER ONE

"You want me to find you a wife? You cannot be serious!"

Vincenzo Angilu Tomasi waited for his personal administrative assistant to close her mouth and stop making sounds like a dying fish gasping for water. He'd never heard her talk in exclamation points, hadn't been sure she was capable of raising her voice, even.

Fifteen years his senior, and usually unflappably confident, Gloria had been with him since he took over at the NY branch of Tomasi Commercial Bank more than a decade ago.

Enzu had never seen this side of her. Had not believed it existed and would be quite happy to put it behind them now.

When she didn't seem inclined to add anything to her shocked outburst, he corrected, "I will provide these children with a *mama*."

Although he was third generation Sicilian in this country, he still gave the old-world accented pronunciation to the word.

His niece, Franca, was only four years old and his nephew, Angilu, a mere eight months. They needed parents, not uninterested caretakers. They needed a mother.

One who would see them raised in a stable environment unlike what he had known as a child or had been able to provide for his younger brother. Which, yes, would mean the woman would have to become his wife as well, but that was of negligible consideration.

"You can't possibly expect me to find them that. It's impossible." Outrage evident in every line of her body, shock dominated Gloria's usually placid-whatever-the-circumstances expression. "I know my job description is more elastic than most, but this is beyond even my purview."

"I assure you I have never been more serious and I refuse to believe anything is beyond your capabilities."

"What about a nanny?" Gloria demanded, clearly unimpressed with the compliment to her skills. "Wouldn't that be a better solution to this unfortunate situation?"

"I do not consider my custody of my niece and nephew an *unfortunate situation,*" Enzu told her, his tone cold.

"No. No. Of course not. I apologize for my wording." But Gloria did not look like she had an alternative description to offer.

In fact, once again, she seemed to be struck entirely speechless.

"I have fired four nannies since I took custody of Franca and Angilu six months ago." And the current caretaker was not looking to last much longer. "They need a *mama.* Someone who will put their welfare ahead of everything else. Someone who will love them."

He had no personal experience with that type of parenting, but he'd spent enough time in Sicily with his family over there. He knew what it was supposed to look like.

"You can't buy love, sir! You just can't."

"I think you will find, Gloria, that indeed *I can.*" Bank President and CEO, the driving force behind its expansion from a regional financial institution to a truly international one and founder of his own Tomasi Enterprises, Enzu was one of wealthiest men in the world.

"Mr. Tomasi—"

"She will have to be educated," Enzu said, interrupting

further ranting on his assistant's part. "A bachelor's degree at least, but not a PhD."

He didn't want someone who was driven to excel academically at that level. Her primary focus would not be on the children but her academic pursuits.

"No doctors?" Gloria asked faintly.

"They hardly keep hours conducive to maintaining the role of primary caregiver for the children. Franca is four, but Angilu is less than a year old and far from being school age."

"I see."

"It goes without saying the candidates cannot have any kind of criminal record; I would prefer they be currently employed in an *appropriate* job. Though the woman I choose will give up her current job in order to care for the children full time."

"Naturally." Sarcasm dripped from Gloria's tone.

That, at least, he was used to.

"Yes, well, no candidate should be younger than twenty-five and no older than her mid-thirties." She *would* have to be his wife as well.

"That narrows down the pool significantly."

Enzu chose to ignore his assistant's mocking words. "Previous experience with children would be preferred, but is not absolutely necessary."

He did realize it was unlikely an educated woman in a career now, unless it was one related to children, would have experience with them.

"Oh, and while I will not immediately rule out someone who has been married previously, she cannot have her own children that would compete with Franca and Angilu for attention."

Franca had experienced enough of that sort of neglect and Enzu was determined she never would again.

"The candidates should be passable in the looks department, if not pretty, but definitely no super-model types."

The children had already been subjected to the beautiful but vain and entirely empty-headed Johana as mother and stepmother.

His brother Pinu's taste in women, from his first serious affair, which had resulted in Franca and a mother who had been only too happy to walk away once Enzu met her financial demands, to the wife who had died with him in the crash, had been inarguably abysmal.

This time around Enzu would be choosing the woman and he was confident he could make a far superior decision to the ones Pinu had made in that department.

Gloria did not reply to Enzu's completed list of requirements, so he went on to enumerate the compensation package he'd worked out for the successful candidate.

"There will be both financial and social benefits for the woman taking on this new role. Once both children have reached their majority *without significant critical issues,*" he emphasized, "the *mother* will receive a stipend of ten million dollars. Each year she successfully executes her maternal duties she will receive a salary of $250,000 paid in monthly installments. She will receive an additional monthly allowance to cover all reasonable household and living expenses for her and the children."

"You really are prepared to buy them a mother?" Gloria was back to looking gobsmacked.

"Sì." Hadn't he said so?

"Ten million dollars? Really?"

"As I said, the bonus is dependent on both children reaching their majority without going off the rails. It will be paid when Angilu turns eighteen. But if one of the children chooses to follow in my brother's footsteps, she will still receive half for the successful raising of the other one."

He did realize there was a certain amount of self-will in the path a person chose to take in life. He and his brothers couldn't have been more different, though they'd been raised in almost identical circumstances.

"And she will be your wife as well?"

"*Sì.* In name at least." For the sake of Franca and Angilu's sense of family and stability.

Gloria stood, indicating she was ready to return to her work. "I will see what I can do."

"I have every confidence in your success."

She did not look reassured.

Well, that could have gone better.

Audrey brushed impatiently at the tears that wanted to fall. When had crying ever made a difference?

Neither her tears nor those of her then twelve-year-old brother had made a difference to Carol and Randall Miller. Pleading had only been met with disgusted impatience and implacable resolve unhindered by *any* emotion, much less love.

Maybe she should have waited a few weeks until Christmas and asked then. Weren't people supposed to be filled with charity during the Christmas season? Somehow she didn't think it would make any difference to her parents.

Audrey should have known they weren't going to change their minds now. She'd been an idiot to think that Toby being accepted into the prestigious Engineering School's Bachelor of Science program at MIT would make a difference.

But she hadn't even asked for any financial assistance, just a place for Toby to live while he attended school. If her parents didn't want him commuting to the MIT campus in Cambridge from their Boston home they could have provided living accommodation in one of their many real estate holdings throughout the city.

They'd categorically refused. No money. No help in any way.

Wealthy and emotionally distant, Carol and Randall Miller used the carrot and stick approach to parenting, with an unwavering conviction in the rightness of their opinions and beliefs. When that didn't work, they washed their hands of what they considered failure.

Like they had with her and Toby.

It had nearly broken her brother to be rejected so completely by his parents, but he'd come back from the abyss stronger and determined to succeed and be happy. And, at twelve, he'd had more certainty about what he wanted to do with his life than Audrey at twenty-seven.

She had no grand plan for her life. Nothing beyond raising Toby to believe in himself and to be able to realize his dreams. Audrey's own dreams had been decimated six years ago.

She hadn't just lost the rest of her family when she'd taken Toby in. Audrey's fiancé had broken up with her. Thad hadn't been ready for children, he'd said, not even a mostly self-sufficient young boy.

When her parents withdrew their financial support Audrey had been forced to take out student loans to finish her third year at Barnard, but a final year had been well beyond her means. She'd had no choice but to transfer her credits to the State University of New York and complete her degree there.

She'd had to get a full-time job to support herself and her brother. Time and money constraints meant that it had taken her nearly four years of part-time online coursework to finally get her Bachelor of Arts in English Literature.

Her parents had been right about one thing. It was a supremely impractical degree. But she wasn't sure she would have finished university at all if she hadn't been studying something she loved so much. Her coursework had been her one break from the stresses and challenges of her new life.

She and Toby had that in common. They both loved learning. But he was committed to excelling in a way she never had been.

With a determination her parents should have been proud of, Toby had earned top marks in school and worked on gaining both friends and confidence in his new environment. He'd said he was going to be happy and her brother was one of the most genuinely joyous people she knew.

She couldn't stand the thought of him losing that joy once he realized they simply couldn't make MIT happen.

It wasn't fair. He deserved this chance and Audrey just couldn't see any way to give it to him.

Only the best and the brightest even got considered for MIT, and those who truly stood out among this elite group were accepted. The private research university accepted fewer than ten percent of their applicants for incoming freshmen and transferring from another school was almost impossible.

Which made any plan that had Toby attending a less expensive state school to begin with and moving on to MIT such a remote possibility as not to be considered at all.

Toby hadn't just gotten accepted, either. He'd won a partial scholarship. It was a huge deal. His high school administration and counselor were over the moon, but not Carol and Randall Miller.

They hadn't softened their stance toward their son one bit. The one question they'd asked had been if Toby still claimed to be gay. When Audrey had told them he did, they'd made it clear they wanted nothing more to do with their youngest son. Ever.

Worse, they'd offered her both a return to the family fold and an obscene amount of money, more than she would need to help Toby go to MIT, with two caveats.

The money could not be used for Toby and Audrey had to sever all ties with her baby brother.

That so was not going to happen. They were *family* and to Audrey that word meant something.

But all the will in the world wasn't going to pay for Toby to live his dream and attend MIT.

He wasn't eligible for federal financial aid because until the age of twenty-five, their parents' income would be used to determine his *need*. Even if he had been, MIT was a *very* expensive school. Four years of textbooks alone would pretty much wipe out what Audrey had managed to save for his college expenses over the past six years.

The cost of living in Boston or Cambridge was high as well, leaving no wiggle room for Audrey to make up for the tuition not covered by the partial scholarship.

Audrey was still repaying *her* student loans. Her job at Tomasi Enterprises barely covered their living expenses now that her parents had stopped making the child support payments required by the state. Toby had turned eighteen two months ago, and things had gotten lean, but she wasn't pulling any money from his college fund. No matter what.

The New York housing market was ugly. Even outside the city, where she'd moved with Toby when he first came to live with her. And because she wasn't in a city apartment there was no rent control. Each new lease she'd signed had included a bump in their rent. Their current year's lease was going to be up a month before Toby graduated.

Audrey had no idea how she was going to make the new rent without the child support payments. Finding a cheaper apartment in Toby's school district wasn't happening, either. She'd been looking for the past three months, just to get on a waiting list.

She didn't know what she was going to do, but she wasn't giving up.

She might not have any dreams left, but she still had a boatload of stubborn.

Unable to believe what she'd heard, Audrey remained in her stall in the ladies' room for several minutes after the two senior support staff who had been talking in the outer area left.

The bathrooms in the Tomasi Enterprises building were swank, providing an outer sitting area where female employees could take their breaks or breastfeed their babies in onsite daycare. Vincenzo Tomasi was known for his pro-family stance.

While the man himself was an unashamed workaholic, he expected employees with families to actually have a family life. Many of the company's work-life effectiveness policies made that clear.

And what Audrey had just heard would seem to indicate that Mr. Tomasi took his commitment to family even more seriously than anyone could ever imagine. Seriously? Ten million dollars for raising his children acquired through the recent tragic deaths of his brother and sister-in-law? And $250,000 a year in salary besides?

It sounded too good to be true, but it worried her, too. Because Mr. Tomasi clearly believed he really could *buy* a loving mother. What he was a lot more likely to get was a woman with dollar signs in her eyes.

Like the one who had been listening to his personal administrative assistant complain about her new and *impossible* assignment. From the way she'd talked, it was obvious the other senior support staffer was more than interested in trying to become a billionaire's wife. That didn't mean she would make a good mother.

But putting on a show to get the job? Easy.

After all, how many people in Boston believed Carol Miller was an adoring and proud parent? Audrey was only too aware of how easy it was to put on that kind of show.

She'd been taken in herself, once upon a time.

The two women discussing what Audrey considered Mr. Tomasi's very personal business hadn't bothered to make sure no one was using the toilet stalls and could overhear them.

While the stalls had actual interior wooden doors that reached the floors, they were all open air a foot from the ceiling for ventilation purposes.

Sound carried. Words carried. And Audrey had heard an earful.

* * *

Palms sweaty, heart beating faster than a rock drummer's solo, Audrey stood outside Vincenzo Tomasi's office.

Was she really going to do this?

She'd spent the last three nights tossing and turning, her brother's future and Mr. Tomasi's outrageous plan vying for attention in her brain. Somewhere in the wee hours of that morning she'd come up with a pretty brash plan of her own.

Unquestionably risky, nevertheless if it worked she could give her brother the best Christmas gift ever. The realization of the dream he'd worked so hard for.

Going through with it could also result in her immediate dismissal.

But despite the lessons of the past six years, or maybe even because of them, she had hope. She and Toby had made it this far when their parents had been sure they would crash and burn, returning to the family fold repentant and willing to toe the line.

They'd said as much when she'd gone to them to ask for help for Toby's schooling.

So hope burned hot in her heart.

Hope that maybe fate had smiled on her and Toby for once. That maybe destiny had put Audrey in that bathroom stall at just the right time to overhear the conversation between Gloria and the other staff member.

Hope that maybe Audrey could make a difference not only in her own life, and that of her brother, but for two orphaned children. Maybe she could give them the kind of loving upbringing she'd longed for, the kind that their uncle clearly wanted for them.

It was insane, this plan of hers. No arguing that. And probably Mr. Tomasi was going to laugh her out of his office. But Audrey *had* to try.

If for no other reason than to impart to him just how easily his scheme could end up backfiring and hurting the children he was so obviously trying to protect.

Audrey had considered long and hard about whether to approach Gloria first or Mr. Tomasi directly, but eventually she realized she didn't have a choice. Not if she wanted to give her crazy, dangerous plan a chance of succeeding.

Approaching Gloria meant giving the PAA the chance to turn Audrey down before Mr. Tomasi even heard about her. She couldn't let that happen.

Audrey couldn't ignore the semi-public nature of the discussion in the bathroom, either. After that lack of prudence on Gloria's part in keeping her boss' information private, Audrey had no confidence in anything like real discretion on her own behalf.

After all, Gloria's loyalty to her employer was legendary. She had no such allegiance to Audrey and even less impetus to keep Audrey's brazen suggestion to herself.

So Audrey had had to figure out a way to see the CEO without his PAA present. It wasn't as hard for her as it might have been for someone else who hadn't spent the last four years fixated in hopeless fascination on the man who owned the company where she made her living.

She'd seen pictures of him before transferring to the company headquarters from the bank, but the first time Audrey had caught a glimpse of the gorgeous, driven man herself she'd stopped breathing and that part of her that used to dream became captivated.

She'd watched, paid attention to everything she heard about the CEO. And every fantasy between wakefulness and dreaming Audrey had had in the last four years had starred Vincenzo Angilu Tomasi.

Her hand froze on the door handle as she had the sick worry that maybe this plan of hers was just another one of those.

Only she fulfilled every single one of the requirements the PAA had said Mr. Tomasi had for the *job candidates*. Even so, Audrey was fairly certain Mr. Tomasi was in no way expecting an applicant from the lower floor offices of his own building.

While she'd been born into a family that were themselves considered high society, Audrey couldn't begin to lay claim to that now. She'd attended Barnard for three years, but her degree was from SUNY and the only one of her friends from those days who still kept Audrey in her orbit was Liz.

The roommate who had saved Toby's life.

Besides, while Mr. Tomasi might not want a super-model like his late sister-in-law Johana for the position, he probably wasn't interested in a woman as average as Audrey.

Her long hair the color of chestnuts was several shades lighter than his more exotic espresso-brown, and arrow-straight besides. While the drop-dead gorgeous CEO had Mediterranean-blue eyes, an exciting and unexpected combination with his almost black hair color, Audrey's were the same chocolate-brown as her brother's.

And they didn't shine with Toby's zest for life, either. The responsibilities and work of her adulthood had taken that from her.

She was average in height as well, with curves that weren't going to make any man stop and do a double-take. Not like the six-feet-four-inch corporate king, who looked more like an action movie hero than a CEO.

Audrey knew she wasn't the first or last woman to fall for him at first sight.

He didn't need to settle for average.

Oh, crap. All she was doing was psyching herself out and that wasn't going to help. Not at all. Either she was going to do this, or she wasn't.

Okay, so she had a crush on the man. So sue her. She *wasn't* applying for the position because of it.

She was here because she wanted to make life better for three children who deserved something better than the hand dealt to them. Her brother might be eighteen, but he was still her child in every way that counted. Even if he didn't see things that way.

For his sake, and that of the little ones, Audrey had no choice but to take this chance.

Taking a deep breath, she pushed the door open to Mr. Tomasi's office without knocking.

He was sitting behind his desk, reading some papers spread out in front of him.

"I thought you weren't going to be back for another thirty minutes," he said without looking up from the papers, clearly believing the intruder in his office was his PAA.

Just the sound of his voice froze the breath in her chest, making it impossible to speak.

His head came up when his comment was met with silence. At first his eyes widened in surprised confusion and then narrowed. "It is customary to knock before entering the office of your CEO."

Funny he had no doubt she was an employee, not a client or business associate.

"My name..." She had to stop and swallow to wet her very dry throat. "My name is Audrey Miller, Mr. Tomasi, and I'm here to apply for a position with you."

CHAPTER TWO

ENZU FOUND HIMSELF nonplussed and that never happened.

It had been years since someone had made it past Gloria to importune him for a job or a promotion. In this case promotion it had to be. None but an employee would have made it to this floor in the building without an escort.

It was sheer luck that this woman had come during the one time a week he was in his office and Gloria was not at her desk.

Reading the intelligence in the chocolate-brown eyes gazing at him from lovely, delicate features made him revise that thought. Maybe not luck at all.

This had been planned. He doubted Miss Miller knew about his little-known weakness for chocolate, though. Her beautiful eyes and the determination tinged by vulnerability he saw in them were unexpectedly compelling.

Regardless, he couldn't let this blatant disregard of company policy go unanswered. "There are procedures for applying for a promotion. None of them include importuning your extremely busy CEO."

She flinched at the ice in his voice, but did not let her shoulders slump, or step backward with an apology. "I'm aware. But this particular *job* isn't on the internal promotion and transfer database."

Disappointment coursed through him. It was like *that,* was it? She was hoping to apply for the *job* of his lover. It wasn't the first time this had happened, but it hadn't happened here at work in a very long time.

"I do not keep a mistress on my payroll." He used the insulting word to remind them *both* exactly what kind of calculation had brought Miss Miller here.

Because he found her tempting, and that was shocking enough to make his usually facile brain sluggish.

Besides his love of chocolate, Enzu had a secret passion for old movies. This woman, breaking every company protocol, not to mention good manners, to accost him in his own office, could be the spitting image of his favorite classic movies film star, Audrey Hepburn.

Elegant and refined. Beautiful in an understated way, Audrey Miller had been aptly named.

"I do not want to be your mistress." The quiet vehemence in her voice was hard to mistrust.

He simply raised one brow in question. He could not believe he was prolonging this conversation. He should have sent her packing with a promise to report her actions to her division supervisor already.

"You told Gloria to find you a mother for your children. I'm here to apply for the position."

Shock kept him from speaking for long seconds. "Gloria told you? She thinks you would be an acceptable candidate?" he demanded.

This was not his efficient PAA's style at all. He'd expected a couple of weeks to pass and then a dozen or so dossiers on appropriate candidates to show up on his desk.

This blunt approach to the situation was entirely out of character for Gloria.

"Not precisely, no."

"Then what, precisely?"

"I would prefer not to tell you how I know about the *job* you hope to fill."

That was the second time she'd put an odd, almost disapproving emphasis on the word *job*. Now he knew what she referred to he could almost understand it, but wasn't she here to apply for the position? If so, she couldn't find his methods as unacceptable as her tone seemed to imply.

"Does Gloria know you are here?"

Miss Miller bit her bottom lip and admitted, "No."

"I see."

"I doubt it."

"You do?"

"If you were that insightful you would realize the very real risk to your children in attempting to buy them a loving mother."

"And yet you are here to apply for the job?" he asked with unmasked cynicism.

"Yes."

"Isn't that hypocritical?"

"No."

Disbelief filled him. "No?"

"I know I am prepared to give them what another woman might only promise for a luxurious lifestyle and multimillion-dollar payoff."

"I assure you I did not build an empire without an ability to read people."

"But you are going about this emotionlessly."

"Which should make me even more capable of making the best decision for Franca and Angilu." And why was he having this discussion with a stranger standing uninvited in his office?

"Not when that decision is about the emotion you are hoping to provide for them."

"A woman does not have to *love* them to be *loving* toward them."

"That you believe that only shows how little you know."

"Excuse me?" Ice laced his tone.

She closed her eyes, as if gathering her thoughts. When she opened them he read frustration, even disappointment, but that determination he'd seen there at first hadn't dimmed. "May I sit down?"

What the hell? "You have fifteen minutes."

Something like anger washed over her features, but she crossed the room and sat in one of the sleek leather armchairs facing his modern, oversized executive desk.

When she didn't speak immediately, he found himself demanding impatiently, "Well?"

"You are looking for someone who will make your children the priority in her life, is that right?"

"You keep calling them my children, but you do realize I have custody of them only because their parents are dead?"

"I know, but your desire to give them a loving mother has made me believe you want to fulfill the role of dedicated father. I guess I shouldn't have assumed." She said the last as if she was talking to herself.

"You are not wrong." He would be a better father than Pinu, who had been borderline indifferent to his two offspring.

"Then they are *your* children?"

"Sì."

She nodded, as if in approval of his admission. He should not care, but he found himself pleased by that.

"So back to my question: you want a woman who will put Franca and Angilu first?"

"Yes."

"And you do not think she has to love them to do that?"

"Financial compensation will ensure it."

"Will it?"

"Of course." He understood money and how to wield it.

"And if something comes into her life that is more important than the money you are paying her to pretend the children are a priority?"

He did not like her description of the job. "She will not be pretending."

"If it is for the sake of the money, how can it be anything but pretense?"

"Regardless, I doubt very much that something will come up that would make someone lose sight of ten million dollars."

"Really? What about a husband who is worth thirty million?"

"I am a billionaire."

"Presuming you are married to this woman, there would be an ironclad prenuptial agreement that only provides her with a yearly stipend and a ten-million-dollar payout nearly two decades down the road."

"You are so certain there would be a prenup?" He hadn't mentioned it to Gloria.

"It only makes sense. A man like you isn't going to offer a woman half of your empire under any circumstances, but particularly if she comes into your life as part of a business proposal, no matter how personal the terms might seem."

He inclined his head in acknowledgment of her insight. "There aren't that many marriage-minded multimillionaires out there."

"But moving in your circles will increase her chances of meeting them exponentially."

"I'm not going to get hoodwinked by a gold digger."

"Maybe. But even if you don't, you must realize that while money can be a very compelling motivator, it isn't always the most important one."

There was something about her tone that made him think she not only believed this, but had personal experience. "Few things trump it."

"You'd be surprised."

Audrey—he found it difficult to think of her as Miss Miller—sighed with the kind of weariness that came from a lot more than a single conversation.

"Tell me, do you think Johana Tomasi married your

brother primarily for the lifestyle she could enjoy as his wife?"

Enzu shocked himself by saying honestly, "Yes."

"And yet, by all accounts, she was not a loving mother."

"You investigated my family?" he asked dangerously.

"Are you kidding?" she asked, with a genuine laugh he found altogether too charming. "I'm a senior specialist in your customer service department; I'm hardly in a financial position to hire a private detective. Johana's exploits were tabloid fodder as much after she became a mother as before."

He could not deny that. "What is your point?"

"She had to know that you would pay her handsomely to be a more involved parent."

Both his brother and sister-in-law had known that, but they'd refused his offers of increases in their allowance in exchange for a quieter lifestyle. "She and Pinu saw no point in having access to money if they couldn't spend it on the lifestyle they enjoyed."

"Exactly."

"Whatever you may think of me, I am not an idiot. I have no intention of bringing a woman like that into the children's lives."

"I do not think you're an idiot at all, just maybe naïve."

"I am far from naïve."

"Oh, you are very worldly and brilliant about money and business…"

"But?" he prompted, knowing that was not all to her assessment of him and inexplicably unable to let it lie.

"But you don't understand emotion."

"Emotion is a weakness I cannot afford."

"That might be true, but do you really want to withhold it from Franca and Angilu?"

"I will give them everything they need."

"You will try. But if you hire them a mother, you are

almost guaranteeing the best they will ever know is kindness born of duty to the *job*."

"You came here to apply for that *job* you are so disparaging of. Are you trying to convince me you wouldn't be doing it for the money?"

"No."

"Exactly," he said, with much less satisfaction than he should have felt at her admission.

"But I am also offering to *love* your children, not just treat them lovingly out of duty."

"You cannot promise to love them."

"Of course I can. They are innocent children, left without their parents. How could I not love them?"

He stared at her, incomprehension washing over him. She believed what she was saying, and yet… "You claim another woman would not do the same?"

"I am not other women. I am me. Sure, there are women out there that would love them, too, but would they be the women your PAA finds to offer as candidates?" There could be no question that Audrey didn't believe it.

"Why?"

Audrey's head went back, an impatient sound coming from her. "I've tried to explain it. You and Gloria, you're approaching this whole thing without any emotion. That's almost a guarantee that the women she puts forward and the one you eventually choose will be every bit as emotionless."

"I still do not see the problem with that." Emotion was volatile, impossible to predict with consistent accuracy.

"No, I don't suppose you do." She stood. "I shouldn't have come here."

"On that at least we can agree."

This time Audrey's shoulders slumped and the wince was more pronounced. Without another word she turned toward the door and crossed his office, an air of defeat surrounding her as she made the long trek.

She stopped with her hand on the door handle. "Do I need to start looking for another job?"

"No."

She turned the handle.

"Audrey."

"Yes?" She didn't turn.

"I assume you had more reasons for believing you were an appropriate fit for the position than your self-proclaimed affinity for *emotion?*"

She tensed, but nodded. "I meet the requirements."

"Tell me how you know what those requirements are."

She just shook her head, and he got the impression that even if he threatened the job she clearly wanted to keep she wouldn't give in.

Gloria had to have shared her assignment with Audrey in a moment of indiscretion, but the younger woman wasn't about to throw his PAA under a bus. He had to appreciate the loyalty.

"I will not tell anyone about this discussion," he offered.

She had been misguided, but he had no wish to see her pay with her livelihood for what he was certain was an honest attempt to protect his children.

"Thank you." Her voice was flat, lacking the passion that had infused her arguments for her point of view during their conversation.

She went to leave, but he said her name again.

She stopped without replying.

"Look at me," he ordered, unwilling to be ignored.

She turned, her face as blank as a statue. No weakness, no emotion showed there, and he couldn't help but respect that. She had to be disappointed, even a little afraid that he would go back on his word and get her in trouble with her divisional supervisor.

"It was a pleasure to meet you." They might not agree, but he'd found talking with her more invigorating than with any other woman in a very long time.

"Thank you."

She left, with the door closing quietly behind her, as he tried to make sense of the fact he was more than annoyed she hadn't returned the sentiment. He was bothered.

Gloria checked in when she returned a few minutes later. Their afternoon went much as he had planned for it to. Enzu would have been surprised if it didn't.

But throughout his meetings and other work parts of his discussion with Audrey kept popping up to distract him. The way she'd looked when she said she shouldn't have come to his office, like she was disappointed. In him.

It was not a reaction he was used to. That had to be why he couldn't put it out of his mind.

And it had nothing to do with him putting a note with Audrey Miller's name on Gloria's desk before she left for the evening. Audrey had claimed she fit all of his requirements. If that was true, it would be a poor business decision *not* to include her in the pool of eligible candidates.

His PAA looked up at him quizzically. "What's this for?"

"I want her on the list."

"List?" Gloria asked.

"Women who would make a suitable mother to Franca and Angilu."

Comprehension dawned in Gloria's pale grey gaze. "That list. Will do."

"I expect dossiers for a minimum of six women with complete background checks on my desk next Friday."

"That kind of rush on the background investigation is going to cost."

"And?"

"Nothing. I just didn't want you having a fit when you saw the expense report."

"I do not throw fits," he said with great dignity.

"Call it what you like. So long as you don't have one of

them when you see how much this little plan of yours is going to cost."

"Fine."

"If you don't mind me asking…?" Gloria said before he could return to his office for an evening of work.

"Ask."

"Who is Audrey Miller?"

"You do not know?" Suddenly the sinister implications of Audrey knowing what she did were at the forefront in his mind. "She does work here?"

"She might very well. I don't know every employee of Tomasi Enterprises. Even I am not that efficient."

"Look her up in the employee database."

Gloria gave him a strange look, but did as he asked. An employee file popped up on her screen. The picture wasn't all that recent, and there were shadows of fear in the young woman's eyes that he had not seen today, but it was the same one.

He didn't let his relief show.

She'd been hired six years ago by the bank for their call center. That explained how young she looked in the picture. She'd been twenty-one, which made her twenty-seven now. So, she *did* fulfill that particular requirement.

But how she knew about them was still a mystery.

"You don't know her?" he asked Gloria again.

"No. She doesn't even look familiar. But she works on the third floor."

And employees on the top floors rarely interacted with those on the lower floors.

He opened his mouth to demand how Audrey knew about the position if Gloria hadn't told her, but snapped it shut. That question would lead to more and reveal Audrey's visit to his office, which he'd promised not to do.

Enzu didn't consider a security breach. Like all cautious men in his position, he had his office scanned for listening devices on a weekly basis by a security team he trusted implicitly. No business rival was getting sensitive information from Enzu's own lips.

Gloria must have told someone and that someone had to have passed the information on to Audrey. He would look into it further after his search for a wife...and mother to his children...was over. Someone had shown an egregious lack of discretion, but that could be dealt with later.

After he'd made his choice about the woman he would marry.

He ignored the way his mind returned again to Audrey Miller. She would be *one* of several candidates, not *the* candidate.

Even if his libido might demand otherwise.

CHAPTER THREE

DUMBFOUNDED, AUDREY HUNG up her phone and took off her headset. Someone else could take the next few customer service calls.

Mr. Tomasi's PAA had just made an appointment with Audrey to meet the CEO for an *interview* the following morning.

It had to be for the job of mother to Franca and Angilu. But the way he'd acted he couldn't be interested in her for the position, could he?

Only tomorrow's appointment said otherwise.

Gloria ushered Audrey Miller into Enzu's office.

He flicked a glance to the Rolex on his wrist. Exactly on time.

He mentally marked a tick on this positives column for the customer service specialist who had shown the courage to approach the CEO of her company in an unconventional way in order to apply for an equally unconventional job.

"Ms. Miller, sir," Gloria said.

As if Enzu would forget who the woman was after little more than a week. "Thank you, Gloria."

He eyed Audrey as she crossed the office on unhurried feet, showing more aplomb than most of his upper level managers when called to Enzu's office for a meeting. She wore a knockoff black sheath dress and an open cropped white sweater with black swirls. The pearls around her throat were no doubt *faux,* but they did not look gaudy. Modest heels raised her average height less than two inches.

It was an elegant if inexpensive outfit. Not a sexy one. But Enzu's body reacted like she'd walked into his office wearing nothing at all.

A curse rose to his lips but he bit it back, swallowing the gasp of shock at his immediate physical response just as quickly.

He'd been hard almost the entire time they'd talked last week and it looked like he was going to experience the same phenomenon again. He couldn't remember reacting like this to another woman in years. If ever.

Either he'd allowed too much time to pass since practicing that particular stress-reliever, or this woman was something special. Cynicism directed he lean toward the former.

Audrey moved with an unconscious grace he liked and Enzu allowed himself the minor pleasure of simply watching her finish her journey across his intimidatingly large office. It was one of the many calculated ways he used to establish his dominant role in any meeting that occurred in this room.

Audrey did not appear intimidated.

He found that reaction, or rather lack thereof, intriguing.

She stopped in front of his desk. "Good morning, Mr. Tomasi."

Enzu did not reply immediately, his brain fully engaged with controlling his body's unholy reaction to this woman.

"Thank you for considering me for this position."

Typical, well-used words in an interview, and yet Audrey's sincerity inexplicably touched him.

Her voice was soft, arousing. Not weak.

The subtle strength of a woman. His many summers in Sicily had taught him to appreciate it and never to underestimate the steel that ran through the spine of a woman who had learned to sacrifice for her family.

Unlike most of his Sicily-based family, Enzu had never once heard his great-aunt raise her voice. But there had never been any doubt in his mind who ran the family. His great-uncle could yell with amazing volume, even at eighty. And yet it was the old man's wife whose quiet orders no one in the family dared to disobey.

Enzu's silence must have lasted too long for Audrey's comfort.

Uncertainty glowed in her chocolate gaze as it flicked between him and Gloria, who remained near the door, an assessing look in her pale eyes as she watched the exchange in silence.

Enzu forced himself to speak, allowing none of his response to this interesting woman to show in his voice. "Have a seat, Audrey." He indicated the chair she'd occupied the week prior.

She nodded, silent, and then sat down in a rush as if her legs didn't want to hold her up. The evidence of nervousness on her part surprised him.

"I assume you understand why you are here?"

"You want to interview me for the position of mother to your children?" she asked, her tone implying she found that particular eventuality very difficult to believe.

"Yes."

A sound escaped her. "Oh. Okay." She seemed to relax, though Enzu could not have identified exactly what gave him that impression.

He was as much an expert at reading body language as any psychologist with a PhD. It was a little unnerving to realize he could not pinpoint the change in hers that indicated her more relaxed state.

It occurred to him that this woman would be a challenging adversary across the boardroom table. He would do well not to forget it, either.

"You are still interested in the position?"

"Yes, I am."

"I am glad to hear it."

"You are? I was pretty sure you had no intention of considering me for the position," she offered candidly. "I thought you'd have a stack of files on women you would find a lot more suitable."

"You are not the only candidate, naturally."

"No, of course not." Her perfectly shaped lips twisted wryly.

A sudden inescapable desire to see how they would look swollen from kisses assailed him.

"I'll bring some coffee," Gloria inserted smoothly.

Enzu nodded his approval of that plan, but Audrey turned her head to meet Gloria's eyes. "I'd prefer tea, if it's not too much trouble."

A spark of admiration shone in his PAA's pale gaze. "No trouble at all."

Enzu appreciated Audrey's willingness to assert her own preferences, albeit politely, as well. His years of experience and study of business psychology had taught him that a person who was capable of that combination usually made a reasonable if strong negotiator.

"Thank you." Audrey gave Gloria a small smile before turning back to face Enzu.

The door to his office closed quietly in Gloria's wake.

Enzu glanced down to the interview questions he'd prepared. "Right, then, let's get started."

"Before we do, I have a question for you."

He frowned, irritated. Did she not realize who was doing the interviewing here? Not that he expected her to have no questions of her own, but to insist on having the first one indicated either a lack of understanding of business protocol or significant self-importance.

Curious in spite of himself, he inclined his head.

Serious brown eyes met his. "My brother is gay and he will always be welcome in my home and my life." There was no give in her voice or the square set of her lovely shoulders.

"That is not a question." But it might well explain certain circumstances he had discovered on reading her dossier.

Her hands clenched in her lap. The only indication Audrey was worried about his reaction to her revelation. "Is that a problem for you?"

"Hardly." He might be the controlling and arrogant powerbroker some accused him of being, but Enzu wasn't a bigot.

Her eyes widened, his answer obviously a surprise to her.

"I take it your parents are not as accepting?" That would explain the fact that Audrey had been raising her brother for the past six years despite the fact their very wealthy parents were still living.

"That's putting it mildly."

"So, your brother came to live with you. Why not your older siblings?" She had two, both successful professionals who presumably would have found it much easier to provide for a twelve-year-old boy.

"They share my parents' prejudices."

"That is unfortunate." And unforgivable, in his opinion, but he left that unsaid.

It was the job of parents and older siblings to protect. Enzu had spent a lifetime protecting his younger brother Pinu, but in the end even he could not prevent tragedy.

Audrey shrugged. "It is what it is."

The flat line of her lips and the hardness that briefly masked her features said Audrey was not as insouciant in the face of her family's betrayal of the youngest child as she appeared.

"Is this also the reason your parents cut you off financially halfway through your junior year at uni?" He'd been trying to figure out the dynamics that had led to that set of circumstances.

She'd been attending one of the most prestigious and one of the few remaining female-only institutions of higher learning in the country. Her grades had been good. Her behavior exemplary. Her known associates had all been from good families with no hint of scandal to their names.

There was no record or even hint of inappropriate behavior on Audrey's part that might have caused such a move on the part of her parents.

"Yes."

"You were forced to get a job?" At *his* family's bank. For some reason the fact that his bank had given her the means to support herself and her brother pleased Enzu. "You had to transfer from Barnard to the state university in your final year and pursue your degree part-time?"

"Yes."

"That could not have been easy." In any aspect. "And still you chose to take Tobias in."

For a moment anger burned in her dark gaze. "He would have ended up in foster care or living on the street. Would you have let that happen to your younger brother?"

"No." He'd tried to protect Pinu even from himself. Grief pierced Enzu.

"I'm sorry." Sincerity and honest sympathy infused her tone and demeanor. "I should not have said that."

"It is truth. Tobias is a lucky young man to have you for his sister."

"Toby. He hates Tobias."

No doubt because it was their father's middle name.

Enzu allowed his lips to curve in a half-smile. "Duly noted."

"Toby is my family." Her tone implied an *only* in there.

He could not blame her for the sentiment. "I find your loyalty and tenacity in the face of the many challenges you've faced admirable."

"Just how detailed is that dossier?" she asked with an edge of annoyance.

"Very," Gloria answered for him as she placed tea things on the table beside Audrey. "Tomasi Enterprises employ only the best. The investigative firm we use knows how exacting Mr. Tomasi's standards are."

Far from looking impressed, Audrey was clearly disgruntled. "I don't suppose it occurred to you to simply ask me about my life?"

"You might lie. My investigator has no impetus to do so."

"I guess most men as high up on the corporate ladder as you are cynical." Again, Audrey didn't sound particularly impressed by that observation.

He took his coffee, already prepared to his specifications, from Gloria. "In my experience, that is true."

Audrey opened her mouth to reply and then seemed to think better of her words. She focused on putting sugar and just a dash of milk into her teacup before pouring the hot beverage.

"What were you going to say?" he asked, curious.

If nothing else, he had not yet found himself bored in this woman's company. He could not say that about a great many people he was forced to spend time with in the name of business.

Her brow furrowed in thought. "It's just that I'm not sure I see the point of this interview if you already know all the answers to your questions."

He almost smiled, but held the expression in. She had no idea how much a simple meeting could reveal, even if the only thing discussed was the temperature outside.

"You do not think it is important to establish whether or not there could be a possible rapport between us?"

"Well, if you had the children here, that particular consideration would make more sense."

"You do realize that being their mother mandates also becoming my wife?"

Or hadn't she?

Was it possible that, however she had learned about the position, Audrey had not been made aware of that particular aspect? The stunned expression on her lovely features implied just that.

She jolted, setting the teacup down without taking the sip she'd planned. "What?"

"Surely you can see that you must be my wife in order to actually be their mother?"

"I hadn't thought about that."

"Does the knowledge mean you would like to withdraw your application for the position?" he asked, with no doubt about the answer.

Who would not want to be married to a billionaire?

To his chagrin and grudging appreciation, Audrey took several moments to consider the question.

Finally she said, "Not immediately, no."

He frowned, less than pleased.

"I'm sorry if that offends you. I just hadn't considered…"

Her voice trailed off and he realized Audrey was seriously rattled.

"Yes, well, consider it."

She nodded, still looking a little dazed. "You're not looking for a real wife, though? Right?"

"The woman I choose will share my home, my family and many aspects of my life. In what way is that not real?"

"Oh, I…uh…I just thought…" Her lovely features went an interesting shade of pink before something seemed to occur to her and they paled to an alarming level.

Nonplussed that the idea of becoming his wife was more daunting to her than parenting two small children, he asked, "Are you all right?"

"Y-ye…" She cleared her throat. "I mean, yes."

He watched with interest as she lifted the teacup in trembling hands to take a sip.

Her eyes closed and she took another sip and several

deep breaths before carefully placing the cup down again. "Um...does that mean you're expecting...uh...*conjugal* relations?"

Humor vied with a vicious spike of arousal at the thought of sharing a bed with Audrey and her reaction to the concept.

The prospect did not send most women into stuttering panic. He was surprised she was reacting so gauchely to the idea. Was it possible she did not feel the passion sparking a steadily building electric current between them?

Or was it that she felt it and was overwhelmed by it? She was twenty-seven years old, not some blushing virgin, though.

"Naturally I would expect to have sex with my wife." He did not mention that he'd actually had no intention of any such thing until this very moment.

But he'd had a sudden and inescapable self-revelation. No way could he live in the same house as this woman and not act on the desire she evoked in him.

Shortsighted of him not to realize the efficiency of such an arrangement as well, regardless of who he chose for the role. Enzu wasn't usually a shortsighted man.

"I didn't realize. I'm not... Well, you probably already know." She gave him an appealing look. "I'm sure it's in that invasive report. Your top-notch investigators wouldn't have left something like that out. Right?"

Enzu was unacquainted with the level of confusion he experienced at her disjointed words. "What exactly are you talking about?"

"My... That I'm a..." She didn't finish her thought.

Enzu found himself more intrigued than confused. That she was a *what?*

An idea came to him. One he dismissed almost immediately as impossible. She was twenty-seven, had attended university, and raised her own brother for the past six years.

Still, considering how little information on that front

there was in the report, he could not help wondering. He had thought she was simply more private in this area than anyone he'd ever come across. Even himself.

And Enzu made it a policy *never* to get his name splashed across the tabloids for his sexual liaisons.

There was no evidence of any kind of sex life in the report on Audrey, but that didn't mean she did not have one. An investigator would find it difficult, if not impossible, to name Enzu's sexual partners in the past year.

"Your discretion in that area bodes well for your ability to maintain my confidences."

Enzu had no intention of *telling* his wife sensitive information, but living together in the same house for at least two decades risked her being exposed anyway.

Audrey was back to blushing and looking into her teacup as if it held the secrets of the universe. "I am a very private person."

"I had surmised that."

"But it's not so much a matter of discretion as there being *nothing* to be discreet about," she admitted, almost as if she was embarrassed by that fact.

He was glad to hear she wasn't promiscuous, but he did not want her to think he expected her to have no past sexual experiences. He was not a Neanderthal.

"I find sex a satisfactory stress-reliever but, like you, I do not indulge as often as some might expect." Enzu wasn't celibate by any stretch, but he was not and never had been a player like his brother, either.

He worked sixty-hour weeks, rarely taking days off— even on the weekend; Enzu didn't have time for a lover, or even frequent hook-ups.

Audrey winced, cherry-red washing over her cheeks. "I don't indulge *at all*."

"Not at all?" he asked with some measure of disbelief.

"Not ever," she admitted, as if it was painful to do so. "I'll understand if you want to end the interview right here.

It was a reasonable assumption that I would have at least some experience."

He wasn't sure why she thought he'd want to cut short the interview, but he was a lot more interested in her claim of total inexperience than just *why* she thought he would see it as a strike against her.

Strangely, the urgency of his physical attraction to Audrey only increased at the knowledge of her innocence.

"You're saying you are a virgin?"

"Yes."

"But you were engaged." The relationship had ended shortly after Toby moved in with his sister. A formal retraction had even been printed in the paper.

"We were waiting until our wedding night."

"People still do that?" he asked, bemused.

"To hear my parents tell it, anyone with a conscience does."

"They seem to be rather narrow-minded."

"You think?" she asked with some sarcasm. "They're also hypocrites. My oldest sister was born seven months after their wedding day. And she was not a preemie, no matter what my mom claimed later."

Enzu laughed cynically. "While your virginity comes as a surprise, your parents' double standard does not."

Audrey nodded and then rose gracefully to her feet. "Right. I appreciate you considering me. I hope you find someone suited to both you and the children."

He stood, too, coming around his desk and blocking an easy exit from his office. "This interview isn't over."

"It's not?" Her forward momentum had taken her to within inches of him before she stopped.

Her scent, a soft floral fragrance, teased his senses. Arousal spiked through him and he had to control the urge to reach out and touch. "No. Surely you realize that it is *my* responsibility to determine when this interview is over?"

"Yes, of course." She stepped back.

He followed her.

Chocolate-brown eyes widened, but she didn't try moving back again. Perhaps she realized to do so might well trip her backward into her chair in a less than dignified manner.

"I have several more things to discuss with you."

She swallowed, her gaze stuck on his mouth in a gratifying way. The attraction was *not* one-sided. He smiled.

She inhaled sharply and then shook her head, like she was trying to clear it. "But I thought..."

"It would take an insecure man to be intimidated by a lack of experience in his possible future sex partner."

"Oh."

The breathy little sound went straight to his sex. "Do you think I am insecure man, Audrey?"

CHAPTER FOUR

"Um, no." Her gaze strayed up to his and then back down to his lips, as if she couldn't help herself.

Would it be so bad to include a kiss as part of the initial interview? This position was hardly typical, or covered under usual human resources procedures.

It was only the fact that the interview had already gone so far awry from his prepared agenda that kept him from giving in to further modification to the plan. He was still in control of this meeting. And himself.

"Do I seem intimidated?" he asked, driving the point home.

Audrey licked her lips and gave a small laugh. "Definitely not."

"Then it appears this interview is *not* over." He gently but firmly grasped her shoulders and guided her back to her seat. "I will tell you when we are finished, *sì?*"

"Yes. Okay. That would be good."

Forcing himself to release her, he stepped back. *"Sì."*

"You were born here in the U.S., weren't you?"

"Yes."

"So why do you say *sì* sometimes?"

"I'm not sure. I grew up visiting Sicily every summer and we did not speak English at home."

"Is your mother of Italian descent as well?"

"No. And our family is Sicilian."

"Isn't that the same?"

"Not to a Sicilian."

She grinned. "I see."

"Bene." He used the Sicilian for good just to make her smile again.

It worked and he was inexplicably pleased.

"So, your mother learned *Sicilian?*"

"Not well, but then my parents were rarely home."

"Your grandparents raised you?"

"The answer to that question is complicated."

"Do I get to use that reply?"

"No."

She looked at him patiently but with clear purpose.

"You are stubborn, I think."

"Maybe."

There was no maybe about it. "My grandmother was from the Old Country. By the time I was born she spent most of the year *visiting* our family in Palermo. My grandfather ran the bank."

"So, you're saying no one really raised you at all?"

He shrugged. "It was better for Pinu."

"Because you tried to help raise him?"

"For all the good it did. I could not give him a loving mother, or a father…just a bossy big brother."

"You're determined his children will have a better childhood than he did," she said with uncomfortable insight.

She realized he wasn't trying to improve on his own childhood, only on what he'd been able to give Pinu.

"Sì."

"I think it's a good thing."

But he saw doubts in her eyes. "You still do not believe I can *hire* a woman to fulfill that role?"

"You're wrong."

"Oh, am I?" he asked, in a tone his senior management would recognize as dangerous.

"Yes. I have no doubt you can entice a woman to marry

you and play the role of mother to Franca and Angilu, especially with the remuneration you are offering—"

"But?"

"But, as I told you last week, I question whether that woman will offer them genuine affection. Children know the difference."

"You are so sure?"

"Yes. Long before my parents played their we-don't-have-a-gay-son card, both Toby and I knew that they didn't feel the same way about us as they did our older siblings, the children they'd planned for."

This was not a conversation he wanted to revisit, so he did not reply with agreement or denial to her implication that Franca and Angilu might suffer the same fate.

Leaning back against his desk, one ankle crossed over the other, Enzu asked, "Are you still determined to wait for marriage before having sex?"

As topic-changers went, it was a resounding success.

Audrey inhaled her sip of tea and had a short coughing fit before demanding, "What? Why would you ask that?"

"Because in addition to having a rapport with the children, my wife and I will have to be sexually compatible."

"You plan on having sex with all the candidates for the position?" Audrey asked with not a little amount of disgust.

He would hazard that not a single other woman on the list of candidates would object to his doing so. However, instead of being annoyed with her for the disapproval set in every line of her body, he found it ridiculously charming.

The truth was, he had no desire to have sex with a bevy of strangers. A man with his wealth and influence could not afford to indulge indiscriminately.

"No, Audrey. Once I have narrowed the candidates down to the most likely hire, she will be introduced to the children in a series of planned meetings. She will also spend time with me, testing our social and sexual compatibility."

"You're talking about choosing a wife like an employee."

"Exactly." He'd always done very well choosing employees.

In the thirteen years since taking over the bank presidency from his father at the tender age of twenty-three Enzu had made exactly four bad hires. He had learned from each mistake.

"You're not normal, you know that?"

"On the contrary, business arrangements for this sort of thing are very common in my world."

"And they're amazingly successful, are they?"

He let Audrey know with a severe look that he did not appreciate her levity.

She frowned back. "What if I don't like the idea of going on a sexual test-drive?"

"I'm afraid it's a non-negotiable." While he had not considered this aspect previously, now that he had he wasn't going to compromise on it.

"But that's not legal. You can't require sex for a job."

"Absolutely, but as much as we are handling this situation like I'm hiring an employee, I am not actually doing so. You won't be working for Tomasi Enterprises or the bank. You will be my wife and the children's mother. Your job here is in no way dependent on what happens in this interview, or later between us, for that matter."

"That's not true."

Shock coursed through him, followed by hot anger he refused to allow to the surface. "You are accusing me of lying?"

"Not exactly. It's just that if I were to be selected as your wife and the children's mother, I believe you would expect me to quit my job."

"That is correct."

"So..."

"Ultimately a successful outcome on your part regarding this position *would* impact your current job, but only in the same way that getting a promotion would do so."

She nodded, still looking a little shell-shocked.

"However, should you withdraw from the application process it will not impact your current or future success with Tomasi Enterprises, or the bank should you transfer back there."

"By 'withdraw' you mean…"

"Refuse the physical aspect." He would not mince words.

"I… This is insane."

"On the contrary; it is efficient."

Her lovely dark eyes narrowed. "You do realize it is illegal to pay for sex in the state of New York?"

Offended, he glared at her, unable to suppress his anger at that particular accusation. "I am not paying for sex."

"It sure sounds like it to me. $250,000 a year."

"That money is to ensure that, as my wife and the children's mother, you would not feel the need to embark on a career to provide an independent income. Many men provide their wives with a significant personal allowance for this very reason."

"Maybe in your tax bracket they do."

Since he had very little experience with life outside his tax bracket, he did not argue the point.

Audrey fiddled with her teacup, but didn't take a drink. "So, this sex thing is a deal-breaker for you?"

"Sì."

She went silent for several long seconds, then seemed to come to a decision. He waited with unaccustomed agitation to find out what that was.

"I think you better kiss me."

"What?" Had he heard correctly? "You want me to kiss you?"

"Yes."

"Why?"

"I think that would be obvious."

He was not used to people implying he was thick. "Explain it to me."

"Because if we don't have the chemistry to make it through a single kiss, the rest of this interview is an exercise in futility. Since you're so set on us being physically compatible."

It actually made sense, and he had not considered it because he'd been so intent on *not* giving in to his urge to kiss her.

He nodded and stood up, away from the desk, putting his hand out to her. "That is an excellent point."

She stared at his hand as if she couldn't imagine why it was there, but with only the briefest hesitation she placed her palm against his. The simple touch jolted the underlying buzz of arousal that had not abated since she'd entered the office.

Curling his fingers around her hand, he pulled her to her feet, her body coming within inches of his own.

Their gazes locked, hers filled with trepidation and something else that he had been unsure he would find there: desire.

"You want me."

"I want a kiss," she corrected, but the truth was there.

He wouldn't ignore the fear, though. The knowledge that this kiss was a test for *both* of them made him determined to make it the best she'd ever had. He could not afford to frighten her with overwhelming passion, but he had to show her that the potential to burn up the sheets between them was there.

Not a man who suffered self-doubt, he confidently cupped the back of her head. Using his hold there, and on her hand, he pulled her forward so their bodies touched.

She gasped, her eyes glazing with passion before he even had a chance to bring their mouths together. How had this woman stayed a virgin for so long?

Enzu bent forward and brushed his lips against hers in the gentlest of caresses. Breath escaped her, leaving her mouth parted. That was when he kissed her.

He did not use his tongue, not yet, but concentrated on giving pleasure with chaste lips. Lust rolled through him in inescapable waves, his body going tense with the need to do more than simply kiss.

She made a soft sound of need and he could not help deepening the kiss, pulling her body hard against him. She had to feel his arousal, but she didn't try to back away. She moved against him in an unconscious invitation that took all of his formidable self-control not to accept.

He wanted her naked on the pristine white plush pile carpet of his office.

Knowing that was impossible, and very much afraid he might do it anyway, he forced himself to gentle the kiss and then pull away.

She moaned in protest, her hand coming up to pull his head back down to hers.

He let her have her way and kissed her again, tasting her desire and the English afternoon tea she'd been drinking. He didn't think the sweetness of her mouth had anything to do with the sugar she'd put in it, though.

She hadn't touched him and he was seconds away from coming in his trousers. Enzu *did not* lose control like this. Not even during the earthiest sex with a highly experienced partner.

Alien fear made him push her away, all the way back into her chair.

She looked up at him with passion-clouded eyes, her lips every bit as enticing swollen from his kisses as he'd thought they would be. "I… That was…"

"Yes, it was." He could not help the harshness in his tone.

He was fighting urges that had no place in a work day.

Her gaze slid down to the revealing bulge in trousers tailored too well to hide his need when it was this strong.

"Yes, I want you." He gritted his teeth, refusing to show any embarrassment at the blatant proof of his sexual need.

"You will agree that our chemistry is strong enough to move forward with the interview?"

For a long moment he didn't think she would answer. He wasn't even sure she understood his question.

But finally she nodded. "The interview. Right. Yes, we should continue."

He wasn't running when he returned to his chair behind the oversized executive desk and the privacy it afforded. Enzu did not run. Nor did he grimace at the pain sitting down with a marble-hard erection caused him.

Audrey collapsed on the sofa in the small but welcoming apartment she shared with her brother.

Totally gobsmacked and exhausted by the "interview" she'd had with Vincenzo, she'd begged off the rest of the day from work. She wasn't going to think of him as Mr. Tomasi after that kiss, or while the threat of test-drive sex hung in the air between them.

Wow. That kiss.

She'd never experienced anything like it. She and Thad had been engaged for two years, and come close to breaking their commitment to wait for marriage, but nothing they'd done together had affected her like Vincenzo's kiss.

The man knew what he was doing with his lips. She hadn't wanted it to end. *Audrey had acted with complete wanton abandon.* If it had been up to her they would have still been kissing—and probably doing it without all their clothes on—when Gloria came in to refresh their beverages and remind Vincenzo about his ten-thirty appointment.

He'd told his PAA to reschedule and resumed his exhausting and often invasive questions. All with a dispassionate air that completely belied the ardent kiss they'd shared.

He'd acted like it had been nothing. Maybe for him it had been. He was probably used to getting that worked up.

No doubt he wasn't still suffering from the frustration of unrequited lust.

Her body, on the other hand, was buzzing with physical desires she'd never felt this strongly. Was it because she was a twenty-seven-year-old virgin? Or was it because the man who'd kissed her was Vincenzo Tomasi, the subject of her most secret fantasies?

With no answer she wanted to acknowledge to that question, Audrey tried to go over the rest of the interview in her mind with as little emotion as he'd shown after their kiss.

Thankfully she had several hours to decompress and think about her meeting with the arrogant man.

Toby had football practice after school and wouldn't be home until later. The season was almost over, but Audrey didn't expect to see much more of him than she did now before Christmas break. He had a full and varied social and academic life. She couldn't have been more proud. Audrey had always been a little shy, but Toby wasn't. Not even a little.

He was personable, confident and so intelligent she was in awe of his brain. Considering what he'd gone through, that was pretty much a miracle.

She wasn't entirely sure how her little brother would react to Vincenzo, though. And the idea of them meeting was a much stronger possibility after the morning she'd spent with the CEO.

The kiss had proved their chemistry and the interview had lasted into lunchtime, culminating in his request that she sign a non-disclosure agreement that covered situations beyond that on the papers that she'd signed for her initial employment with his bank. Vincenzo had left his office to give instructions to Gloria for the paperwork.

The PAA had returned only a few minutes after Vincenzo with documents for Audrey to sign.

Rattled from the kiss and the interview that had followed it, Audrey probably hadn't taken as long looking over the documents as she should have. However, after noting that the first few paragraphs were identical to the non-disclosure agreement she'd signed when hired on to his company, she'd found herself skimming the rest when the words blurred together in her brain anyway.

She did note that the agreement forbade her discussing the whole *hiring a mother for his children* thing and she'd had no problem signing it.

By that point she'd just wanted to get out of the office and as far away from the emotions Vincenzo Tomasi provoked in her as she could.

He'd quizzed her on every aspect of his *requirements* for the position, plus a lot more besides.

While he had agreed that on paper Audrey seemed to meet them all, Vincenzo wanted deeper clarification.

She'd expected him to bring up the issue of Toby, since one of the requirements was that she not have any children of her own. When he didn't, she did. But Vincenzo had dismissed the apparent conflict, citing Toby's age and his plans to go off to college the following fall.

He did not deny that for all intents and purposes Audrey was Toby's mom, despite their only having a nine-year age-gap between them. He assured her that he realized Toby was part of the Audrey Miller package.

Vincenzo's concerns seemed weighted toward her willingness to be an "at-home mom" and give up her career.

Since Audrey had never considered her job as anything but a way to support herself and Toby, she felt no qualms about leaving it. If she'd had a career she was passionate about, that would have been something different. For Toby's sake she might have been willing to put even that on hiatus, but as it stood Audrey had no major barriers between her and fulfilling a requirement Vincenzo obviously considered very important.

She wasn't really sure why Vincenzo was so stuck on a dedicated full-time mother for his niece and nephew.

She thought it might be a knee-jerk reaction to losing his brother and sister-in-law.

He'd decided what would mitigate that loss the most for the children and was determined to provide it.

She thought it might be different if any of the grandparents were active participants in the children's lives, but they weren't. Johana's parents lived in Germany and visited the States rarely. They'd never even met their grandson Angilu.

And Vincenzo's parents appeared to be a lot more like his late brother Pinu than Vincenzo, constantly traveling and pursuing fun like it was the elixir of the universe.

Maybe Vincenzo was trying to create the family he had not had growing up, even if the powerful businessman did not realize it.

And that was all well and good. Audrey did not object to being a dedicated full-time parent. In fact she looked forward to it, having lost that personal dream like all the others when Thad walked away.

But the sex…Vincenzo's plan to test out that particular compatibility…had Audrey's stomach tied in knots. Even more so now that she realized how strongly he affected her physically. In a word, it *terrified* her.

She was embarrassingly susceptible where he was concerned.

What happened if she became addicted to his lovemaking and he decided it wasn't good enough with her?

Her deepest fear lay in the possibility that her inexperience and lack of practical knowledge in that area might bore him, if it didn't turn him off completely.

His clinical attitude toward sex between them, or rather him and the most promising candidate, was really off-putting, too. Especially after he'd kissed her to within an inch of her life.

What virgin wanted her first time to be some kind of test-drive for compatibility?

CHAPTER FIVE

ENZU WAS SURPRISED at his own impatience as he waited for the driver to collect Audrey.

In the car parked outside her apartment building, Enzu was ostensibly going through emails on his tablet. He found himself looking out the window instead, watching for her arrival.

It wasn't a new complex, but the buildings were maintained, as were the grounds. A group of teenagers played basketball at the end of the parking lot.

If he was not mistaken, one of those young men was Audrey's brother. The tall, heavily muscled teen matched the pictures in her dossier. Grabbing the ball he was dribbling, he stopped, and his head came around to face the direction of Enzu's car.

The teen waved and yelled something and Enzu realized he'd missed Audrey's arrival. She called out a goodbye to her brother as the driver opened the door nearest her. Audrey paused before getting into the car, her body tense.

At least thirty seconds went by and she did not move, her jean-clad legs showing no indication they would be bending in the imminent future.

Enzu stifled the urge to call her name. There were times for putting a subordinate in place for keeping him waiting. This was not one of them.

His impatience did not stem from his schedule. It was

caused by his desire to see her again. To give in would be to show weakness, a loss of control that would be unacceptable. Enzu was discovering the chocolate depths of Audrey's eyes to be even more addictive than the sweets he indulged in rarely but enjoyed thoroughly.

No, his life was governed by an iron will backed up by careful planning. He did not get surprised; he did not become impatient waiting for something he wanted. Enzu was a rock and everyone around him knew it.

His reputation for being able to wait without urgency for a business rival to slip up, or a meticulously thought-out plan to increase his company's holdings to bear fruit, was legendary.

He could most certainly wait for one rather innocent woman to get into the car.

A moment later Audrey did just that, settling into the seat beside him as the driver closed the door.

"Good morning, Vincenzo," she said, without looking at him as she buckled her seat belt, only the slightest tremble underlying her tone to indicate she wasn't feeling as breezy as she acted. "It's nice and warm in here. I don't think I need this." Audrey tugged on the sleeves of her black peacoat, shrugging it off along with a houndstooth scarf. "I hate wearing a coat for long drives."

"We have that in common." He was in his shirtsleeves and tie.

Enzu had removed his suit jacket before leaving Manhattan and had the driver place it along with his overcoat on the empty front passenger seat.

"Would you like to put your coat in the front?" he asked, when it became clear she meant to put it on the seat between them.

For some reason Enzu did not like the idea of the cloth barrier.

She took far longer to answer than a question so simple

should warrant. Perhaps she was as attached to the buffer as he was bothered by it.

In the end she assented, however. They went through the process of passing the peacoat through the accessibility panel to the driver.

Enzu slid the thickly paneled glass back into place, affording them a measure of privacy. The driver would not hear what was said, and the glass was reflective on his side, though not perfectly opaque. Particularly at night, when a light was on in the backseat for Enzu to work.

They were on their way when Enzu asked carefully, *"Vincenzo?"*

That finally brought her too addictive gaze to his. Instead of looking self-conscious at the familiarity, she frowned. "Really? You are going to suggest I should call you Mr. Tomasi when meeting your children?"

Audrey didn't mention the kiss, earning his respect— even if it was only prompted by the shyness of innocence. Either way, plainly Audrey wasn't trying to trade on their explosive attraction. Most women whom he had shared any sort of intimacy with expected to get something out of it, satisfying orgasms notwithstanding.

Audrey had some other point to make by using his first name that she patently expected him not only to understand but to agree with. He'd found this happening several times during their interview.

It should annoy, but instead her honest and often black-and-white viewpoint fascinated him.

As an international business and power-broker, Enzu found his reality had a lot more shades of gray.

"Their nanny calls me Mr. Tomasi," he pointed out.

"But you aren't hiring a nanny, are you?" She seemed to be trying to read something in his face, with no indication if she'd found what she was seeking. "You're looking for a wife who will be their mother."

"You have a point."

He could feel her mentally rolling her eyes, even though she didn't allow her expression to go there. It suddenly struck him that although Audrey Miller had undeniable trepidation about sex, she wasn't actually afraid of *him*. She hadn't been intimidated the first time she approached him and that hadn't changed.

Even with $250,000 a year and a ten-million-dollar bonus on the line.

This woman was definitely unique.

"I am used to my employees being in awe of me."

She laughed like he was joking. "None of your other employees has the prospect of a sexual compatibility test-drive hanging over their head. Do they?"

"Of course not." And he had no idea what that had to do with the way she approached him as just any other man. "And the prospect should hardly be seen as the Sword of Damocles by you, either."

"Says the man who uses sex as a stress-reliever. You know you could just take up Judo, or something. Join a gym."

Enzu surprised himself with an unfettered laugh. "I'll take the sex, thanks. And I already work out six days a week."

"Six? I let Toby push me into running with him three times a week and that's plenty. What are you? Obsessed?"

"Not hardly." But Enzu's lifestyle had the natural by-product of an excess of adrenaline. A solid cardio and weight regime helped him manage it. Enzu had no intention of having a heart attack before he was forty.

"It's a surprise you have energy left over for sex."

"I promise I do."

She huffed out something he didn't quite catch.

It might have been something about an oversexed throw-back, but he wasn't going to ask her to repeat it. "You will enjoy it, I promise you."

"That remains to be seen."

He had a sudden urge to kiss that prim look right off her lovely features. He could not help remembering just how much they would both enjoy that. "I think we proved prospects are good already."

She opened her mouth, shook her head and closed it again.

He waited to see what would come out next.

"How long is the drive to your house?" Audrey asked, clearly ready to put the subject of sex to rest.

"Ninety minutes."

"That can't be convenient."

He shrugged. "I can work in the car. When I am in a hurry I use the helicopter."

"Still, a three-hour commute every day has to be murder."

"I only go to the house on the weekends. The top floor of Tomasi Enterprises is divided into three apartments. Mine takes half of the building space and the two smaller ones are used for business."

"You only see the children on the weekends?" Audrey asked, her tone shocked and not a little disapproving.

"I assure you this is not an uncommon practice in my world." Hell, he would hazard that her own father hadn't made it home to their Boston mansion every night during the work week.

"But who takes care of them during the week?"

"Currently a nanny. But if you will remember the answer to that question is why we are currently in this car together."

"But children need to see *both* of their parents—when they have them—on a much more frequent basis. Especially when they are so young."

"You are suddenly an expert in childhood development?" he asked, with more humor than irritation.

She grinned, the sweet humor coming over her features absolutely arresting. "Research. One thing a degree in English Literature is good for...? Learning how to research."

"You've been studying how to parent small children?" he asked, impressed.

"How else was I supposed to figure it out? I suppose I could take classes. They offer them now pretty commonly."

"Your own mother's example isn't one you want to follow?"

"I don't remember how she parented me as a small child, but, no, I don't think I'd want to leave my children to the nanny and the housekeeper like she did Toby."

"No. That's exactly what I'm hoping to avoid for Franca and Angilu."

Of the six women he'd interviewed he was certain Audrey was the only one who had taken a proactive approach to preparing herself for the actual nature of the job. His decision to single her out for introduction to the children was proving to be the right one.

"It pleases me that you've taken this initiative."

"I'm not in the habit of going into situations blind if I can help it."

"We have that in common as well."

She laughed, the sound wry. "You take the control-slash-prep thing to heights well beyond me."

"I see my reputation precedes me."

"Yes. Your attention to detail and insistence on controlling every aspect of a venture is not exactly a secret." A soft rose washed over her cheeks, but didn't deepen into a full blush.

What was that about? Did she think he would mind that she'd done some of that research she was so adept at on him?

Or did she think he was controlling in the bedroom too? That might disconcert a virgin. However, there could be no denying that his reputation for control in that area was well-earned as well.

Audrey would come to appreciate it, he was sure.

"I hope I'm dressed all right," she said, in a clumsy bid to change the subject. "Mother always said a lady's wardrobe didn't include a pair of jeans, but I live in them outside the office."

Enzu took in Audrey's form-fitting jeans and the tangerine sweater with a scooped neckline that hinted at modest curves. Her trainers weren't brand-new, but they didn't look over-worn, either.

She wore only a small pair of gold earrings, no other jewelry, and had pulled her silky brown hair up into a ponytail.

It was a more casual look than he was used to among the women of his acquaintance, but he couldn't say he found it displeasing. "I do not think the children will care."

"No, I suppose not." She gave him a very serious look from her melting chocolate eyes. "I haven't forgotten what we were talking about."

Funny, he'd thought she wanted to. "Oh?"

"If you live in the city during the week, then the children should also live there."

Okay, *he* had forgotten that discussion.

"You cannot be serious?" He could not imagine two small children in his sleekly modern penthouse.

"I am if you are."

"What does that mean?"

"If you are as committed to being your niece and nephew's *dad* as you expect the woman you hire to be their *mom,* then you'll do whatever is in your power to see them as often as possible."

"Children need a place to play, to be able to go outside."

"So take them to the park. Create a rooftop garden, if the building doesn't have one already. You're a billionaire. You've got options."

He was disconcerted to discover he realized she was

right. He did have options, if he was willing to look outside the box. And apparently Audrey *was*.

He ruthlessly stomped down the urge to reach out and touch this amazing woman. "You didn't have options. Six years ago."

"No. I didn't." Old pain flared in her eyes, then disappeared just as quickly. "But I did my best for Toby with what I had."

"You did an excellent job, by all accounts."

"You investigated Toby too?" she asked, and then shook her head. "Of course you did."

"It's no small thing he's won a scholarship to MIT."

"It's partial."

"Yes."

And dependent on Tobias completing his senior year with a full courseload of advanced classes and a near-perfect grade point average.

Considering how well the young man had done thus far, Enzu had no doubts on that score. Apparently the prestigious university didn't, either.

"He is the reason you want this position, isn't he?" It was the only key issue they hadn't touched on in the interview.

Generally Enzu preferred to draw his own conclusions about people's motivations. If asked, they often lied. However, he found he wanted confirmation of his suppositions in her case.

"Partly, yes."

"Your parents refuse to help with his schooling?" he asked.

"They wouldn't have paid child support if the state hadn't forced them."

"That is criminal." Enzu might have been born in the United States, but his family was Sicilian and he'd spent every summer in the Old Country until he'd started working at the bank.

Even then he'd spent several weeks a year with his extended family.

A Sicilian took care of his children. No exceptions. His father and brother might not have gotten the memo, but Enzu had.

A Sicilian who had the chance to send his child to a good school? He sacrificed whatever was necessary to do so, just as his great-great-grandfather had done for his own son, paving the way for the foundation of their family's current fortune.

The Millers weren't rich like Enzu, but they *were* wealthy and could easily afford to send their son to MIT without the scholarship.

Audrey let out a low, bitter laugh. "I always thought so, but I've learned one thing about my parents. If they can't control their children, that is considered failure, and failure is unacceptable. Better to write it off completely."

"Were they always like that?"

"I didn't notice so much as a child, but then I lived in my own world of books and make-believe." She sighed. "They were always cold, hard to please. I don't remember them ever telling us they loved us, so I should not be surprised it turned out that they didn't."

"And yet they had four children?"

"The first two were planned and exactly to spec. I was Mother's *oops* baby of her thirties and Toby was her *little accident* in her forties."

"No child is an *oops* or an *accident*." Enzu was outraged on her behalf.

His parents were self-serving and allergic to responsibility, but they had never made him feel like they would rather he'd not have been conceived, much less born. Quite the opposite, in fact.

Enzu was certain that his father had been planning for the day he could abdicate his business responsibilities to his son from the day of Enzu's birth.

"I agree, but then as the official *oops* I'm prejudiced in my thinking."

"Franca is not Johana's child." Enzu had not meant to admit that, but eventually he would have to tell Audrey if she turned out to be the successful candidate.

That eventuality was looking more and more likely.

"I know. They didn't even start dating until three years ago."

"You've done your own research."

"Are you surprised?"

"No. More impressed."

"Funny. I find your dossier on me invasive."

"Perhaps I am too used to being the focus of unrelenting interest."

"Your brother and parents spend a lot more time in the forefront of the media."

"It takes a great deal of effort and foresight on my part to keep my own affairs private."

"That explains it."

"Explains what?"

"Why there's all sorts of information about the business exploits of the man who took over his family bank's presidency at twenty-three and became a billionaire by the time he was thirty-five. But no girlfriends. No exploits."

"I do not indulge in girlfriends or exploits worthy of media attention."

"Or if you do you do a very good job of hiding your involvement."

"For instance?"

"Tomasi Enterprises funnels financial resources into a fund that has donated significant amounts to disaster relief ever since the levies broke in New Orleans."

"How did you find that out?"

"I told you, research. The study of English Literature requires a fine ability to follow obscure references and threadbare connections."

"I see. I guess it's a good thing the media sharks that target me weren't English Lit majors."

"Why not let people know about your company's generosity? Wouldn't that be good for the bottom line?"

"We have an official charitable donation fund."

"But it's a lot smaller than the amounts you've given in secret."

"If it weren't, Tomasi Enterprises would be inundated with requests for money. We aren't the Red Cross."

"I think you're a lot of things you pretend not to be."

Audrey's expression worried him a little. "Do not make me into a hero. I am not. If you forget the basic truth that I am at heart a ruthless businessman, you will get hurt."

"And you don't want that?"

"No."

"That's not exactly ruthless."

"I didn't say that if my interests and yours collided I would not hurt you, only that it would be my preference not to."

"I'll try and remember that."

He did not like the humor underlying her tone. "Do."

"Tell me how you ended up the bank's president at twenty-three."

"My father abdicated."

"But didn't he only take over from your grandfather a few years before that?"

She really had done her research. "Yes. Grandfather's heart precluded him continuing in the position. I do not think either of them wanted my father in the chain of command."

"Because your father is more interested in having fun than in making the money that makes that fun possible?"

"You have a way with words."

"That's how I became a customer service specialist."

"I imagine our clients find you a soothing presence on the other end of the phoneline."

Audrey grimaced. "Most of the time, yes. Some people are just plain cranky."

No doubt. "I tend to expect perfection."

"I'm sure you get it."

"Most of the time." He repeated her words.

She smiled. "You didn't really answer my question."

"I did."

"No, you explained the chain of events that led to you being bank president right out of graduate school, but not how you made that work. Most twentysomethings would have ended up sending the bank under."

"I worked summers and weekends at the bank since my fourteenth birthday. And then I interned in management while getting my MBA from Columbia. You could say I was raised in the bank."

"You never acted like you didn't want the responsibility, but it couldn't have been easy watching your brother get to enjoy his youth in a way you never did. Heck, your father was partying up like a twenty-three-year-old when you were busy saving the family fortune."

"Why should I have complained?" Enzu asked in genuine confusion. "I always *wanted* to take over the bank."

"Why?"

Audrey had more insight than most, and Enzu wasn't sure how he felt about that, but he answered her question with candor. "It was painful to watch it languish under my father's leadership. Even my grandfather ignored opportunity after opportunity to grow the business. He was too busy catering to a limited clientele with ties back in Sicily."

The Sicilian branch, Banca Commerciale di Tomasi, had been the beginning of the bank, but that didn't mean it had to continue to be the mainstay institution.

He added, "Tomasi Commercial Bank has always prided itself on being accessible to its Sicilian brethren, but today the American side is far more diversified and international."

"So you had plans to expand the bank from the beginning?" she asked, sounding like she found it hard to imagine someone of his age with those aspirations.

"When I took over, Tomasi Commercial Bank had only three branches on the East Coast. Within three years of me stepping up to the helm we had branches of the bank in all of the biggest U.S. cities."

"Is that when you turned the day-to-day operations for the bank over to a team of senior level managers?"

He was no longer surprised by the depth of her research. "*Sì*. I still guide financial policies and major investments for the bank, but I'm able to keep my involvement down to a once-a-week conference call and the occasional meeting."

"That's kind of incredible."

"It was necessary in order to do what I really wanted."

"Start Tomasi Enterprises?"

"Yes."

The bank provided for his family, keeping them in the lifestyle they were so certain they deserved. But Enzu had wanted more. He'd wanted something that was his alone. So, he'd taken a loan out against his stock in the bank and started Tomasi Enterprises.

"And now you are applying the same brilliant brain that made you a thirty-five-year-old billionaire to finding a loving and attentive mom for Franca and Angilu?"

"That is the hope."

"I think maybe I want you to kiss me again, Vincenzo Tomasi."

"My business acumen turns you on?" She wouldn't be the first woman that had happened to.

His power was more an aphrodisiac than his money for many women.

"Your commitment to putting the same energy into making the children's life a good one that you do your business melts my heart."

"I'm not looking for your heart. You need to understand that."

Audrey didn't look surprised, or particularly worried. "You may just get it anyway."

He shook his head, but bit back the compulsion to argue. She'd offered a kiss and no one could accuse Enzu Tomasi of failing to take advantage of a good thing.

"I think it might be easier if you slid this way."

She unbuckled her seat belt and moved to the center seat, redoing the seat belt before turning to face him, innocent desire darkening her beautiful brown eyes. "Well?"

He was smiling when his lips met hers.

CHAPTER SIX

IT TOOK NO time at all for Audrey to simply melt under the caress of Vincenzo's lips.

His expert lovemaking made her own lack of experience a moot point. And it was lovemaking. Regardless of what she'd intended when she asked him for this, it was no simple kiss.

His mouth conquered hers, drawing forth a response that came from the very core of her. Not just her body, though she yearned for a physical intimacy she'd never known, but to the place inside where she'd always believed her soul resided.

How could she feel so hot, so needy and so profoundly *moved* at the same time?

It had never been like this with Thad. They'd been in love, or so she'd believed, but nothing they had done together had blown her away like Vincenzo's kiss.

His hands cradled her head, his lips molded to hers, his tongue only barely brushed the place where they met, and yet her entire body thrummed with a buzz of indescribable pleasure.

The kiss in his office had been amazing, like waking up after years of going through life asleep to her own sensuality. But this? It was beyond that. It was colors coming back into her world she hadn't even realized had faded away.

It was drenching sensation. His high-end cologne

smelled familiar, but it was changed by his own scent enough she could not name the brand. The texture of his lips reminded her that mouths were made for more than talking.

A tantalizing sensation she could not get enough of— the slick glide of his tongue against the seam of her lips, releasing the hint of Vincenzo's unique flavor—taunted her to open her mouth and get more.

And she had thought it could not get better than their last kiss, that maybe she'd even built that kiss up in her memory.

This kiss, so much more powerful than the first, decimated any thoughts in that direction.

Perhaps pleasure built on itself? She didn't remember that happening with Thad, but then it had been six years, and she'd done her best to forget the past so she could live in the present.

Audrey moved restlessly, straining against her seat belt, needing to be closer.

Vincenzo seemed to understand, sliding his arm out from under the shoulder harness to lean over her. His big, warm body pressed hers back into the luxury car's seat.

Her nipples peaked, drawing impossibly tight and pressing against the silky fabric of her bra with pleasure so acute it was almost painful.

Vincenzo's hand slipped down Audrey's body and under the hem of her sweater to caress her stomach. Long masculine fingers spread possessively, causing every centimeter of skin he touched to grow scorchingly hot from each spark that lit her nerve endings.

Her own hands went to his broad shoulders and then slid down and around his back, reveling in the feel of the well-honed muscles bunching under her touch.

She moaned, long and low—no hope of keeping the unmistakably sexual sound inside. A small voice of reason tried to tell Audrey she should be embarrassed by that. She wasn't promiscuous, that voice insisted.

A much stronger voice, the one he'd woken with that first kiss in her office, insisted this felt much too good to be worried about sounding like a woman who couldn't wait for that test-drive Vincenzo had demanded.

His hand drifted up her stomach, over her ribs, stopping only when his thumb rested in the shallow valley between her breasts and his forefinger barely pressed the underside of one curve. That hand just stayed there, tempting, taunting with what it might do next.

Her own fingers clutched the fine fabric of his dress shirt, fisting it in a way that was bound to leave wrinkles.

With a deep groan that rolled through her like a touch, Vincenzo pulled his lips from Audrey.

He tipped his head back, though his upper torso remained pressed against hers, that tormenting hand still resting intimately against her skin. "We have to stop."

She shook her head. No. She did not want to stop. "More kissing." *More touching*.

The sound that came out of him was deeply pained, his gaze flaring with blue fire…the hottest part of the flame.

Unable to stop herself even if she'd wanted to, and she so did not, Audrey strained forward. She could barely reach to match her mouth to his again. Their lips barely touched.

And that was way more arousing than she'd ever thought such barely there intimacy could be.

His head dipped toward hers, and her entire body sighed with relief at the contact.

Only the kiss did not deepen. He did not move his lips against hers. He was warring with himself; the conflict was so intense she could feel it.

As the seconds dragged on the tension emanating from him grew until he was like a perfect sculpture in marble, his breathing the only movement Audrey could discern.

Then, so slowly she felt the withdrawal of his lips in increments, Vincenzo pulled his head back again. "No, *biddùzza*. We cannot continue."

"Why?" How could he want to put the brakes on such amazing pleasure? Unless he was used to that depth of feeling—or, worse...it hadn't been as good for him. "Did I do it wrong?"

His laugh was harsh, his square Sicilian jaw rigid. "If you had done it any more *right,* I would have embarrassed myself."

"Why would you be embarrassed?" That didn't make any sense.

His sardonic expression said she should know exactly what he meant. When she gave no indication that she'd gotten it, because...well...she *hadn't,* his gaze flicked down their bodies.

Hers followed and even she couldn't miss the impressive bulge that had to be pressing painfully against his zipper.

Only then did the implication of his words sink in. "Oh."

"Sì—oh."

"But—"

"Your first time will not be in the back of a car with only the illusion of privacy."

"My first time? You thought...you want...?"

"Sì, I *want, biddùzza.* Very much."

"Biddùzza?"

"Sicilian."

"For?" she prompted.

"There is no precise translation."

"Really?" She wasn't buying it. She'd look it up on the net if he didn't tell her.

He huffed out a breath that could have been irritated or amused. "It means beautiful, but is a more intimate endearment than *bèdda.*"

"Not so hard to translate after all."

He shrugged, giving off an uncomfortable vibe she didn't associate with such a self-possessed man.

What was it about explaining it to her bothered him? Italian men used *bella* all the time. It didn't mean anything.

She was sure it was the same for Sicilian men with *bèdda.* Only he hadn't called her *bèdda,* had he? He'd used a more personal endearment.

She blinked up at him, her mind working. "Do you call other women *biddùzza?*"

"No." Firm. Sure. Even a little scandalized at the idea.

So it was special for her. And unintentional. Which meant the American-born Sicilian tycoon was not as in control as he appeared.

Warmth suffused her being, delight increasing the sexual need thrumming through her. She let her body shift down so his fingers shifted up, covering the underside of her breast. Her nipple ached with the need to be touched as well, but she just stopped herself from slouching into the seat so that could happen.

Vincenzo's breaths were suddenly coming in more rapid gusts between them. "Stop, Audrey."

"I'm not doing anything." Very much. "You're the one with your hand… Well, you know."

He couldn't expect her to ignore that, or the way his big, toned body pressed into hers.

Vincenzo flashed a shark-like grin that was anything but comforting.

"This hand?" he asked, brushing the thumb of his left hand—the one safely cradling her head—down along her neck.

"You know it's not." Though it seemed to be more of a threat to her equilibrium than she'd suspected.

That simple caress revealed the direct line between that tender spot on her neck and the place between her legs clamoring most for his attention.

More than the sensual onslaught, there was something entirely possessive about the way he held her head just where he wanted. Something that said no matter what he might be feeling, regardless of small cracks in his near-impenetrable armor, Vincenzo Tomasi was in control.

Of himself. Of her.

A moment of clarity sent frissons of uncertainty through her. Could she spend the better part of two decades, perhaps even longer, as this man's lawfully wedded wife?

The overwhelming desire to do just that would have taken her legs out from under her if she were standing, it was so powerful.

"You must mean this one?"

He was still playing the sensual game while she'd been having her life-altering internal revelation.

He let one finger slide up to brush over her nipple, bringing Audrey instantly back into their hot, sensual bubble.

This man was lethal. "Y-yes, that one."

He chuckled darkly and moved the overstimulating appendage down her stomach. Slowly. So very slowly. Neither of them made the tiniest sound as he withdrew his hand from under her sweater.

He carefully tugged the hem into place before sitting up. "You are a temptation."

"But you stopped."

"It is for the best."

"According to your plan," she teased.

"It is my habit to follow my plans."

"You never lose patience and just do something because you want to?"

"No."

No room for misinterpretation there. "One thing I've never heard anyone call you is impulsive."

"My cautious nature has served me well."

"You and your company, not to mention Tomasi Commercial Bank."

Vincenzo had pushed the bank to withdraw from high-risk, high-yield bonds before the stockmarket tanked.

His bank and company had suffered minimal damage while the rest of the financial world teetered on the edge of bankruptcy.

"I used to be impulsive." When there had been room in her life for spontaneity.

His expression was tinged with disbelief. *"Used to be?"*

"You think I'm impetuous?"

"Sì." One word. No clarification. Absolute certainty.

"I'm not." She couldn't afford to be anymore.

"You do not think coming to my office with no introduction or any idea of how I would react to your initiative to apply for an extremely unorthodox position was impulsive?"

She frowned, unable to actually deny the charge. She *had* had no idea how Vincenzo would react to her. Audrey could have lost her job that day, or at the very least gotten a severe reprimand.

"Desperate times…"

"And was it desperate times that made you ask me to kiss you in my office and again just now?"

"Not desperation, no."

"Did you *plan* to kiss me then or today?"

"No." Today she'd meant to get to know two small children to whom she might well become a mother.

"You see? Impulsive."

"But you kissed me both times."

"While I may not share your impetuous nature, I am a man who knows how to take advantage of a fortuitous circumstance when it arises." He sounded entirely too smug.

"You think an opportunity to kiss is lucky? I would have thought you had plenty of those you turned down all the time."

"In that you would be right, but you have left out the key element to the equation."

"What is that?"

"The opportunity was to kiss *you,* Audrey."

Wow. She didn't know how to respond to that. He'd implied that she was something special, but she wasn't. Just one of several candidates he was considering for a position she was coming to want more and more.

"You're sort of lethally charming, you know?"

"You would be one of only a few who think so."

She just shook her head at such a ridiculous claim.

"I am a workaholic who has spent most of my adult life building a financial empire, not a charming playboy."

Like his brother Pinu. And his father, whose affairs were legendary and legion despite his being married to the same woman for almost four decades.

"If a kiss affects me like this, I'm afraid your *test-drive* is going to kill me," she jokingly admitted.

"I fully intend for you to experience a surfeit of *la petite mort,* I promise you."

The promise of multiple orgasms sent shivers of reaction through her. This man pushed every single one of Audrey's buttons.

Just as she'd warned him, her heart was engaging at light speed, her four-year crush fast becoming something else. No matter that he wasn't interested in her emotions. She had no more choice about that than how quickly her body responded to his kiss.

She wasn't sure she believed in love at first sight, but Audrey would never forget her first glimpse of this powerful man. He'd been to the bank for a meeting. Her heart had ended up in her throat and hadn't dislodged itself until an hour later.

She'd applied for a transfer to Tomasi Enterprises a week later and told herself it was for the bump in pay and responsibilities.

Audrey had spent four years watching him from afar, reading every article that was published in the printed and electronic press about the brilliant business tycoon. She'd saved the link to a rare interview he'd given which had been uploaded to the net in her Favorites.

He'd fascinated her. This man who could take apart a

company with ruthless precision for maximum financial gain, but who had personally driven his own corporate policies that benefitted not only his employees but their families. His charitable contributions were evidence that, no matter how cold and emotionless Vincenzo Angilu Tomasi might appear, his heart was as human as anyone else's.

She only wished it was accessible to her. But that was one miracle she had no hope of.

Audrey didn't know what she would do if Vincenzo chose one of the other candidates to complete his little family. However, there was an undeniable part of her that hoped fervently he did just that.

The fear he would choose her was almost as strong as the fear he wouldn't, and Audrey had the inescapable feeling her heart was going to end up broken either way.

"I should move back to the other seat."

He adjusted his seat belt across his torso. "Don't. It gives me satisfaction to challenge my control."

If she were more confident in her own sensuality it might make her happy to add to that challenge. To spend the rest of the ride teasing him in subtle ways, until maybe that control even broke. Perhaps someday, when she was not a sexual novice.

As it stood, she did her best to bring her own clamoring desires back to manageable levels.

"How did you accomplish the Gatling coup last year?" she asked, pretty sure that the discussion of acquisitions and mergers would be staid enough to help in that endeavor.

What followed was actually both interesting and informative, and not just about that particular financial windfall Vincenzo had engineered. His answer revealed both the power magnate's passion for his work, and a great deal about his personal business philosophy as well.

"So, you try to keep a company active if you can?"

"It depends on the numbers."

"What do you mean?"

"If I can realize a minimum of a ten percent return on investment within a year, or twenty-five percent within three."

"So if you only project a nine-point-seven ROI, you dismantle and sell?"

"*Sì.*"

"What if selling for parts wouldn't net you the minimum ten percent either?"

"Then I would not have bought it."

"So, no exceptions?"

"No."

"But you can't be sure about those numbers. I wasn't a business major, but even I know that there has to be a margin for error with any income projection." She worked for a financial institution after all.

She couldn't help picking up a thing or two.

"Naturally. However, that margin is taken into consideration and is far narrower for me than it might be for someone else."

"You don't lack confidence, that's for sure."

"Should I?" he asked, arrogance lacing his tone, and his expression just this side of condescending. "I built a multimillion-dollar investment into a billion-dollar company in less than a decade, during a worldwide financial slump the like of which has not been seen in decades."

"When you put it like that…" She grinned, inviting him to share her self-deprecating acknowledgement of his undeniable financial genius.

He returned the smile, his blue eyes warming in a way that was way too appealing for her peace of mind.

They arrived at his house a few minutes later. Wrought-iron gates swung inward to allow the car through, closing with only a small clang behind them.

The winding drive was so long Audrey did not see the house until they crested a rise after the first curve. A brick mansion that would have made royalty proud rose toward the sky, its windows indicating there were three floors aboveground and no doubt one below as well.

"Full-time mother does not include housekeeping duties?" she asked faintly, entirely daunted by the prospect of keeping up with such a huge property.

"Not at all. There is a full-time housekeeper who oversees a team of maids."

"Sounds like a hotel."

"No. It sounds like a home. My home."

Oh, she'd hit a nerve with that one. She hadn't meant to. "I'm sorry, Vincenzo. I didn't mean to imply it wasn't a lovely place to live."

"Enzu."

"What?"

"My family calls me Enzu."

Audrey didn't point out that she wasn't a member of his family, or that she wasn't even sure she ever would be. She was too busy swallowing down the emotion his invitation to use the nickname engendered in her.

She just nodded.

"The housekeeper does not live in. She and her husband, the groundskeeper, have a small cottage on the property. They are usually in the house from early morning until just before dinner."

"Oh." Audrey wasn't sure what to say to that.

This lifestyle was entirely outside her experience.

Yes, Audrey's mother had a part-time housekeeper who kept her home immaculately clean and running smoothly, as well as a cook. But that wasn't anything like having a bevy of staff charged with keeping this impressive mansion a pleasant home for a billionaire and his newly acquired children.

"Devon serves dinner. Because he likes to." Tolerant affection laced Vincenzo's tone.

"Who is Devon?"

"He is my majordomo."

"You have a majordomo?" She should not be surprised. Vincenzo needed someone with ultimate authority over his domiciles, considering the fact one was a mansion on its own estate and the other a penthouse apartment in the city.

Her research had not revealed other properties, but that didn't mean Vincenzo didn't have any. As that was not of particular interest, Audrey hadn't dug that deep.

"Devon worked for my parents when I was a child and came to oversee my household when I left the family home."

Audrey heard what she wasn't even sure Vincenzo knew he was saying. If she hoped to come into that household and make a place for herself, she'd do well to make a friend of Devon.

"He lives in?" she asked, pretty sure she already knew the answer.

"He, the cook and a night-shift maid are the only ones that do." Vincenzo frowned. "And the nanny, Mrs. Percy."

"You don't like the nanny?"

"She's competent."

"But?"

"She is…" Vincenzo's gorgeous blue eyes narrowed in thought. "Cold. A little emotionless."

It was all Audrey could do to stifle laughter at the irony of Vincenzo Tomasi labeling someone else as emotionless.

CHAPTER SEVEN

ENZU WATCHED IN pleased amazement as Audrey coaxed his quiet Franca right out of her shell, drawing forth smiles the little girl usually reserved for those she knew well.

He'd been startled when the first thing Audrey had done was to drop to her haunches when she was introduced to Franca, bringing herself down to eye-level.

Enzu often did the same, but that was because he was over six feet tall and did not want to intimidate his diminutive niece. Audrey was hardly a giant for a woman and yet she made the same concession.

She'd put her hand out to shake and waited patiently with an encouraging smile for Franca to shake it. Enzu had been shocked when Franca had done just that.

And the surprises just kept coming.

Audrey was currently sitting on the floor of the playroom, coloring with the four-year-old. Enzu found himself doing what he often did with the children: sitting back as he watched in silence.

He'd taken a seat at the table meant for coloring, but apparently Audrey and Franca preferred the floor.

Audrey laid a new blank piece of paper out between them. "What do you think we should draw now?"

They'd started with people. Franca had drawn a very wobbly stick figure with a square that was supposed to be a computer. She'd said it was Uncle Enzu. Working.

Audrey had praised the picture, but given Enzu a look he didn't want to interpret. He was pretty sure there'd been a component of disapproval and maybe even pity.

"Flowers?" Franca asked uncertainly.

Audrey's enthusiastic agreement had Franca's tense shoulders relaxing and soon they were coloring again. His niece made yellow and pink shapes that vaguely resembled circles with green lines going toward the bottom of the paper. The stems, no doubt.

Audrey drew a single bloom that filled the whole sheet, a big daisy with fat petals and a tiny stem, but exaggerated leaves. She then proceeded to color each fat petal in a truly bizarre fashion.

"Flowers don't have polka dots," Franca whispered in a worried tone to Audrey.

"In our imagination they can be anything we want."

Franca looked askance at Audrey. "Johana said flowers had to be pretty."

Everything inside Enzu froze as he waited for Audrey to respond to Franca's first mention of her dead stepmother since the accident had taken Johana and Pinu from her.

"Did she?" Audrey asked in an offhand manner.

Enzu let out a breath he was just now conscious of holding.

Franca nodded somberly. "She said my flowers weren't pretty enough to keep." Remembered hurt was reflected in the small features. "Johana always threw my pictures away. Percy keeps them. In a special frame."

Enzu's jaw hardened and his less than stellar view of his late sister-in-law dropped another notch, while another tick went in the column of why he had to keep Mrs. Percy on. While the woman always seemed cold toward *him,* it was clear she did not react to her charges the same way.

Audrey stiffened, but her tone remained relaxed. "Maybe she didn't understand art. Some people don't."

"Art?"

"Your pictures are art."

"They are?" Franca asked, eyes the same blue as Enzu's wide with wonder.

"Absolutely. Some people don't realize that art doesn't always look exactly like its inspiration."

"What's inspiration?"

There were an extra couple of syllables in the word that made Enzu smile.

Audrey smiled, too. "Like the flower you're thinking of when you draw one. Or how you remember seeing your uncle working so you drew him."

"Oh. I've got a book about flowers. They're so pretty."

"I'd love to see that book if you want to show it to me."

Franca jumped up. "I'll go get it. It's in the library. Uncle Enzu has shelves just for us."

She was running from the room before Audrey could answer.

Audrey turned troubled eyes to Enzu. "I know I've just met Franca, and I could be jumping to conclusions, but I don't think Johana was the most sympathetic stepmother around."

"My brother had questionable taste in women."

A snort from near the door told Enzu the nanny had returned. "It's not my place to say, I'm sure, but I've been caring for that little tyke for a month now and I'd say your assessment was spot-on, Miss Miller."

Enzu wasn't surprised when the nanny didn't address him directly. She rarely spoke to him. He was pretty sure it wasn't because she was intimidated by his wealth and position, either.

The woman didn't approve of him. He would have fired her after the first week if Franca and Angilu hadn't responded so well to this expatriate Scottish woman of an age to be their grandmother, if a youngish one. Besides, Devon approved of her, and he had shared Enzu's disgust with the other nannies he'd fired.

Audrey just nodded in acknowledgement of the nanny's words. "Has Angilu woken from his nap, Mrs. Percy?"

"You can drop the Mrs., my dear. My families just call me Percy."

She'd never asked Enzu to drop the *Mrs.* and it was news to him that her *families* called her Percy.

He'd thought Franca did so because she found it difficult to remember the *Mrs.,* and Enzu had been unwilling to press the point of manners when the little girl was in such a fragile place.

"Thank you, Percy. And please call me Audrey."

"As you say, my dear."

The nanny actually smiled at Audrey, shocking Enzu even further.

Enzu repeated Audrey's question to the older woman. "Is my nephew awake?"

"He'll nap for another bit, if I know the wee tyke." Mrs. Percy directed her words to Audrey. "We've got him on a schedule that keeps him sweet and sleeping through the night finally, the poor bairn."

"Losing his mother would have been traumatizing for him." Audrey made the words sound almost like a question rather than a statement.

"I take leave to doubt that one saw enough of her bairn for him to even know she was his mum."

The words might well be true, but family loyalty forced Enzu to say coldly, "You are hardly in a position to make such a judgment, Mrs. Percy."

"Am I not, Mr. Tomasi? I am no green girl." The nanny shook her head, like she was disappointed in one of her charges. "Do you think I took this assignment without doing my own research about the family I would be in charge of? Chance would be a fine thing."

He couldn't help it. He looked over at Audrey. The humor sparkling in her delicious chocolate gaze at the mention of research made something in his chest hurt.

He met the nanny's eyes. "I am coming to understand that some employees are as committed to doing background research on me as prudence dictates I on them."

"Employees?" Audrey asked, her voice strained, but not with anger.

The woman was laughing at him and making very little effort to hide that fact.

Mrs. Percy drew herself up in truly imposing manner. "I do not consider my role as that of mere employee, Mr. Tomasi."

"What do you consider yourself, then?" he asked, with more curiosity than annoyance.

"The woman charged with raising your children."

"Surely that is their parents' job?"

"Franca and Angilu have no parents."

"What precisely do you consider me?" he asked, in a tone even Gloria and Devon knew to be wary of.

"An uncle who deigns to visit them once a week for a few hours between your all-important work."

"A billion-dollar company does not run itself."

"And children do not raise themselves. Those wee bairns have a barely-there uncle. No father. No mother. Och, it's a cryin' shame, it is."

"I am working to rectify that," he said, more defensively than he'd intended.

"I'm sure we'll all be pleased to see the results of your efforts."

If Mrs. Percy had spoken in sarcasm he would have fired her on the spot. No matter how impressed with her Devon was. But the nanny had actually sounded sincere.

"We will be seeing more of you around here, then?" she asked Audrey.

"Not exactly, Percy," Audrey interjected.

The disappointed resignation in the Scottish woman's expression made Enzu feel guilty, though he had nothing to feel guilty for. And he did not understand Audrey's reply, either.

They *would* be seeing more of her in future. He wasn't making a decision as important as who would be the children's mother without seeing more than a few hours' worth of interaction.

Audrey patted Mrs. Percy's arm and gave Enzu an implacable look. "You and the children will be joining him in the Manhattan apartment during the week from now on."

Enzu was almost amused to see a look of shock in the nanny's eyes matching the feelings that had momentarily frozen his ability to speak. *Almost* being the key word.

"They will?" he demanded in a tone devoid of emotion.

If he let his voice rise at all he would yell. Enzu did not yell.

Audrey didn't have the sense to back down and her expression said so. "We spoke about it in the car. On the way here."

As if he might not remember when they'd been in the car last when it was less than an hour ago.

"Normally I would oppose such an unsettled lifestyle, but those wee bairns need a parent more than they need to live in the same domicile all of the time." Mrs. Percy ignored the tension thrumming between Enzu and Audrey. "As time goes on they'll come to see both the apartment and this house as their homes. So long as the *people* around them remain constant."

"Yes, well…" For the first time in memory Enzu found himself speechless.

He should be lambasting Audrey for making such a pronouncement and explaining to Mrs. Percy that they weren't going to do any such thing. However, he couldn't make the words come.

Because, as furious as he was with Audrey's highhanded pronouncement, it struck him that she might have been right about the children living with him. He should have thought of it himself.

Which just went to show one more reason they needed a mother.

Before he could say anything, in agreement or denouncement, he realized Franca stood in the doorway of the playroom, her book held against her chest with one small fist.

She looked at him imploringly. "Really? We are coming to live with you for *always?*"

"You do live with me."

Franca's little brows drew together in confusion. "No, we live here."

"This is my house." Even as he said the words he realized the ownership of a house meant nothing to a little girl.

Disappointment began to drain the anticipation from Franca's sweet features.

He could not stand it. Dropping to his knees, he looked into the eyes that could have been his own at that age. "Do you *want* to live with me all of the time, *tesoruccio?*"

"Will you be my daddy? My *real* daddy who loves me like the ones in my stories? The daddies who don't go away?"

Enzu would have said he had no heart to break, but he would have been wrong, because something inside his chest shattered at his niece's questions. The pain was so great he could barely breathe.

There was no answer he could give this child but one. *"Sì."*

"My own true papa? You promise?" She reached out, her small hands cupping his face, her expression so solemn.

He could not even force a word from a throat unaccountably tight. So he nodded.

"Say it. Say you promise. I can believe it then."

"I promise," he croaked out, his own voice weak like he'd never heard it.

How could she believe in him after her own father had let her down so completely? And not in death, but in life.

"My old daddy—the one in Heaven now—he never, ever promised to stay. He liked going away."

God in Heaven. Enzu did not think it could hurt anymore. *He* had let this child down. He'd known Pinu wasn't father material, but had wanted to believe that some of what he had taught his brother had stuck.

He had known Pinu liked the whirlwind of constant fun, but Enzu had never considered he would completely ignore the needs of his own child. Not like their parents had done all too often.

"Can I get a *mama* too?" Franca asked in a tiny voice, as if she thought she should not ask for anything else but could not help herself.

Enzu almost laughed, but it would have come out sounding more bitter than amused so he held it in.

"Sì."

It was a vow.

One he would not break. Even if he had not embarked on the search already he would have promised.

His gaze slid to Audrey, whose eyes glistened wetly. Approval shone in her gaze, and her trembling lips curved in a smile too sweet for the likes of him.

"Well, now, that's something. Maybe I've misjudged you, Mr. Tomasi. Maybe I have." Mrs. Percy looked to Audrey and then back at Enzu. "If your plans are what I've an inkling about, you may just have more common sense than I took you to."

Enzu spent the rest of the day learning how to interact with a four-year-old and a baby from experts. The children had been in his care for six months and this was the first time he'd made baby Angilu smile, or interacted with Franca in any meaningful way.

Because of Audrey.

She hadn't raised any children, but the woman so reminiscent to him of the Hollywood legend who bore her name seemed to instinctively know how to react to both Franca and Angilu. Not to mention the prickly nanny, who unbent enough for the first time in a month of weekend visits to actually invite Enzu into the children's activities.

Audrey even gamely changed Angilu's diaper. Enzu did not take things to that extreme.

He enjoyed his time there more than he ever had, and when the hour came for the car to take Audrey back to the city he informed her that she would be taking the helicopter, so she could stay longer.

She gave him a quiet look he could not interpret.

"You do not think you might have asked?"

"It can make no difference to you, surely?" She would be home at the same time.

"What if I get airsick? Or was looking forward to the car-ride to decompress?"

He opened his mouth, but discovered he had no glib answer to those possibilities. "Would you prefer to take the car?"

"No."

"I do not appreciate games, Audrey."

"And I don't play them. But I won't spend the better part of at least the next two decades being treated like a subordinate."

"You are assuming you will be the chosen candidate?"

"On the contrary. I am making darn sure that if you do choose me you know what I expect in the way of treatment."

It made sense and he had to respect her commitment to honesty. She could have let him choose her and then started making demands after the contracts were signed and the vows spoken.

"I am accustomed to making unilateral decisions." Not having them made for him. "Even with my family."

"I imagine they put up with it because they don't want to give up the lifestyle you provide."

He'd often thought the same thing, had in fact maybe even mentioned it on the few occasions his parents, his brother or his wife might have balked at Enzu's directives.

He did not think admitting to that would stand him in good stead with Audrey, though. Enzu merely nodded agreement.

"I won't live that way."

"What way, exactly?" He needed this particular requirement spelled out to him.

"If it affects me, you discuss it with me. You don't tell me the way things are going to be."

"That is not a natural way for me to be."

"Are you admitting you are controlling?"

"Shouldn't I?"

She laughed. "You really are arrogant, aren't you?"

"Sì." He'd never denied it. "I will try to remember to discuss things with you that concern you."

It was a generous concession on his part and he hoped she realized it.

Audrey's expression would indicate that, as Mrs. Percy would say, *chance would be a fine thing.* Nevertheless, she said, "Thank you."

"You will have to remind me when I slip."

"Don't worry, I will." She sounded entirely too pleased with the prospect.

But she'd said she expected to *discuss* his decisions with him, not that she would refuse to adhere to them. He could live with that.

He wondered if she could, once she realized what he had agreed to and what he *hadn't.* That was in the event that he chose *her* for the role of Franca and Angilu's mama.

Not that after today Enzu could imagine deciding on anyone else.

Franca adored Audrey already. Mrs. Percy treated her

like royalty and Devon had given his subtle approval of her as Enzu's friend and guest as well.

"Do you think Devon would be willing to live in Manhattan during the week?" Audrey asked in uncanny synchronicity with Enzu's thoughts.

"I imagine so. He and the cook used to stay with me, but when the children came to live here I put him in charge of the household."

He trusted the older man like he didn't trust anyone else. Enzu was not a man who made friends and his own family had never been on his list of trusted intimates.

"That's wonderful." Audrey beamed at Enzu. "He'll make the weekly transition between homes that much easier on the children."

Speaking of the man himself, Devon came into the family room. "Mrs. Percy has asked me to inform you that the children are ready for their bedtime routine."

"Yes?" Enzu replied.

"I believe she is under the impression you wish to participate. I am quite certain young Miss Franca is expecting you to as well."

"Oh. Yes, we'll be right up." Enzu stood.

Audrey remained seated and was biting her lip.

"Are you coming?"

"Do you think that's wise? The children shouldn't become too attached to me until we've established I'm going to be a permanent fixture in their lives."

He didn't like it, but he grudgingly agreed. "That is a good point."

Enzu didn't understand the look of disappointment that came over her lovely features at his words. Surely she did not expect him to announce right then that he'd chosen her? No, that would not be it. Since he could not decipher it, he chose to ignore it.

"Mr. Enzu?" Devon asked before he could leave the room. The man refused to call him Enzu, and Enzu was adamant he not be addressed as Mr. Tomasi by a man who had known him since childhood. Mr. Enzu was their compromise.

"*Sì?*"

"Mrs. Percy has informed me you plan to bring the children with you to the city?"

"*Sì.*"

"I believe extensive preparations at the apartment will have to be made as it is not in any way a child-safe or friendly environment."

"I will not have the children disappointed." He'd said he was taking them with him on Monday and he would. Well, more likely tomorrow, to give them all a chance to settle in. "We will muddle through."

Audrey gave a disbelieving laugh. "Seriously? If you had a building that needed to be ready to host international meetings on a moment's notice and houseguests, what would you do?"

"Find another building. I am not moving." Not only was the apartment his home, but it was the safest place to live for the children, being on top of the well-secured Tomasi Enterprises building.

"And if using another building was not a choice?"

"I would have the necessary preparations seen to."

"Right. Because you are a freaking billionaire, Enzu. You can hire people to childproof your apartment before you take the children down tomorrow afternoon."

"Who said I was leaving tomorrow? I usually return to the City on Monday."

She just rolled her eyes.

"You should not be able to predict my behavior. You barely know me."

"Sheesh, Enzu. Some things are just common sense."

"Like hiring a crew to prep my apartment?"

"Yes."

Devon cleared his throat. "I believe several pieces of furniture will need to be replaced."

Thinking of the glass and chrome theme prevalent throughout the penthouse, Enzu agreed. "I will give instructions for the removal of all furniture deemed dangerous to a four-year-old and crawling infant."

Devon nodded his approval and Audrey smiled hers.

Enzu let out an exasperated sigh. "If that is all? I believe Mrs. Percy is expecting me."

He might have left without getting a response from either his majordomo or Audrey, but Vincenzo had the distinct feeling he had *not* gotten the last word.

CHAPTER EIGHT

"You were kind of dragging this morning, sis," Toby said as he dug into his full farmer's breakfast.

Audrey shrugged. She'd done pretty well, considering. "I missed my midweek workout."

They'd taken their usual Saturday morning run and followed it with a stop at their favorite diner for their once-a-week indulgence: a traditional breakfast, including eggs, bacon and pancakes in Audrey's case, or very crispy hashbrowns in Toby's. Her brother also added buttered toast with jam, but Audrey would never have been able to eat that much.

As it was, she usually left about half of her pancakes.

"I think this new work schedule is kicking your butt." Toby grinned and winked, looking way too knowing for her *little brother.* "And going out on dates almost every night isn't helping."

If only he knew.

"I was home before you were last night," she pointed out, wanting the focus of the conversation off her.

"Yeah, well, I've been dating since freshman year. You haven't been out with a guy since that jerkwad Thad broke your engagement."

Audrey grimaced, but the pain that would have once accompanied her brother's reminder was thankfully absent. Thad's defection on the heels of her parents' rejection had devastated her in a way she'd never shared with anyone. Least of all her baby brother. He'd taken on enough guilt because of the changes in Audrey's life.

Toby chugged down his orange juice and then set the empty glass on the table. "Too bad your work schedule changed right when you met your superhero."

"Superhero?" Vincenzo *was* larger than life, but a superhero?

"Yeah. He's gotta have superpowers of persuasion to have talked *you* into one date, much less three."

She laughed as her brother had intended. "You might be right."

The last week had passed in a blur for Audrey. Having adjusted her work hours to a seven-to-three schedule at Vincenzo's request, she'd spent nearly every afternoon getting to know Franca and Angilu. Some of which had bled into evenings spent with Vincenzo—sometimes in the company of the children, sometimes not.

Audrey didn't feel guilty telling her brother she'd been out on dates, because that was what they'd felt like. Not an extended interview and personality compatibility test for a really different kind of job.

Vincenzo was a charming and urbane companion, treating her like a woman he wanted to spend time with, not an employee or potentially *convenient* wife. Nevertheless, it was a tiring schedule, and restless sleep wasn't helping, but she couldn't do anything about it.

They had shared more scorching kisses and Audrey's dreams were filled with the heated slide of flesh against flesh. She'd woken aching for something she'd never known more times than she wanted to admit.

"I guess when word comes from down on high, you don't have much choice though, huh?"

"Right." If only Toby knew.

To explain the abrupt change in her schedule, she'd told Toby that her boss had requested it, which was not a lie.

No way was Audrey telling Toby the details of Vincenzo's plan, though. If she ended up as Vincenzo's wife and the children's mother, Audrey's brother was never going to know it was anything but a normal marriage.

"So, when am I going to meet this guy?" Toby pressed after they'd finished their breakfast in silence.

Maybe never. But she couldn't say that. "We're not at that place yet."

Which, again, was not a lie, but not the entire truth, either. Walking this fine line of honesty with her brother was wearing on Audrey even more than the new work schedule.

Toby did not look impressed by her answer. "What *place* do you have to be in for your brother to meet your date and decide if he's good enough for you?"

"I love you to death, Tobe, but no way are you screening my dates."

"You talk like there have been more than one."

"I'm twenty-seven. Definitely old enough to screen my own men."

Her brother snorted. "Not even close. I may be a teenager, but I've dated more guys than you and I can spot across the length of a football field."

"What are you? Super Spotter?"

Toby flexed impressive biceps. "That's me, teenage superhero."

"Better than a teenage werewolf."

They both cracked up and Audrey sent up a silent prayer of thanks for dodging that particular bullet right now.

"You going to be at the game today?" he asked her as they lingered over coffee, letting their big breakfasts settle.

"Of course." No way would she miss it. Not even for another day spent with Vincenzo and the children at his mansion outside the city. "It's your last one."

"Maybe not. I could play in college, depending."

"At MIT? I didn't even know they had a football team."

"Sure they do. The *Engineers*. Fitting, don't you think?"

"Definitely." She grinned and then turned serious. "But I don't know about you playing. Adjusting to your course-work at MIT is going to be a challenge, even for you."

"About MIT, Audrey—"

"No, Toby. Don't you dare say it," she interrupted. "You got in. You got the scholarship. You have to trust that the rest will come together."

"There's a really big stretch from here to the rest coming together. I can get a job, but even I know trying to work full-time and attend MIT isn't going to make it."

"I don't want you working."

"We're not going to have a choice."

"Maybe." She couldn't tell him what she was trying to do to make his dream happen, but she wasn't going to let Toby give up on it, either.

"I applied for more scholarships from independent funds, but the chances of getting a big one is really small, you know?"

She nodded, too choked to speak at first. "Have I told you how proud I am of you?"

"Only like a million times. You're such a *girl,* Audrey." He tried to sound like he was complaining, but Toby couldn't hide his pleased glow.

"I *am* a woman, Tobe."

"Don't remind me. One who's dating, even." He gave an exaggerated shudder.

She rolled her eyes and threw his words back at him. "Don't remind me."

"Right. You gonna bring him to the game?"

She tried to suppress her horror at the very idea of Vincenzo Tomasi at a high school football game, much less meeting Toby before he absolutely had to. "That wasn't my plan, no."

"Yeah, not really convenient, huh?" Toby frowned for just a second. "Wish our last game was a home one."

"There will be plenty of people cheering on your side

of the field. It's not that far away." Only about forty-five minutes north of the city in good traffic.

"Yeah?"

"Yes."

"Maybe you should call your guy and invite him, then, huh?"

Assuming that he was already at the mansion with the children, Audrey did not call Vincenzo.

Not that she would have, regardless. Even if maybe a tiny part of her wished she really was dating Vincenzo and inviting him to watch her brother play football would have been a good idea.

She was making her way around the field to the bleachers for fans of the visiting team when she heard a high-pitched voice yell, "Audrey!"

Stunned, unable to believe she'd heard what she thought, Audrey turned. The sight that met her sent the air exploding from her lungs with the same power of a blow to the chest.

"Franca?" Audrey shook her head, trying to clear her vision.

Obviously she was hearing and seeing things. Maybe the lack of sleep was really getting to her.

But after closing her eyes for a count of five and then opening them again she continued to see the same thing.

Little Franca, bundled up in a pink fur-lined parka and snow boots in deference to New York's chilly November temperatures, stood holding Vincenzo's hand. She looked like a miniature snow bunny.

Audrey couldn't help smiling at the sight.

Highlighting the family resemblance, Vincenzo and Franca wore matching expressions of satisfaction at Audrey's obvious surprise.

"What are you doing here?" Propelled by an irresistible force, she moved toward them. "Where is Angilu?"

"We are here to watch the game with you." Vincenzo's

smile had a predatory edge that was entirely absent in that of his innocent niece.

He was looking stunning in black jeans, ankle boots and a cashmere sweater under a fleece-lined leather jacket. His head was bare and he wore no gloves. Because, unlike normal humans, apparently Vincenzo Tomasi defied even the cold.

"Angi and Percy are at home," Franca informed Audrey. "He's too little to be out in the cold." The small girl was plainly very happy to be considered old enough for the outing.

"Wow. I didn't expect you." Which felt like a huge understatement.

Audrey was completely and totally gobsmacked. She'd been sure that after turning down his invitation to spend the weekend at the mansion she wouldn't see Vincenzo until the following Monday.

"We surprised you," Franca pointed out very happily. "Are you glad?"

Despite Audrey's misgivings about her life with Toby colliding with what was going on between her and Vincenzo, she couldn't say anything but, "Yes, most definitely."

The tiny girl nodded with satisfaction. "Good."

"Shall we find our seats?" Vincenzo asked. "It appears the bleachers are filling quickly."

They were, which would make her brother and the other players on his team very happy.

Bemused, Audrey only nodded.

Somehow she found herself holding Franca's hand. Vincenzo used the arm he rested lightly over Audrey's shoulders to guide them all to a spot near the center of the bleachers about halfway up.

His bodyguards took up positions on either side of the bleachers, another joining them in the stands a little to their left and behind. The security team had made an effort to blend, foregoing their usual dark suits.

It must have worked because no one seemed interested in the three highly trained bodyguards. Vincenzo was another story, however.

Other parents, students and their friends weren't exactly subtle in the avid interest they were showing the gorgeous billionaire.

For his part, Vincenzo seemed oblivious to the scrutiny. Or maybe he was so used to it he took it in his stride.

Audrey wasn't so sanguine. And when the parents of Toby's teammates jockeyed for introductions she was relieved that Vincenzo took care of it himself.

"Vincenzo Tomasi," he said, offering his hand to shake to the men around them. "This is my daughter, Franca."

At that, the little girl positively glowed.

"Are you a friend of Audrey's?" one of the football moms asked.

"Yes," Vincenzo answered simply, showing no compulsion to add details such as Audrey would have felt.

Details that would have tangled her thoughts, not to mention her tongue.

One of the dads asked Vincenzo, "So this is Toby's first game you've seen?"

"It is." Again no further explanation.

The man was good.

"You must be the new guy Audrey's dating," said Brian, Toby's best friend of the non-football-playing variety.

"You are one of Toby's good friends?" Vincenzo asked without answering.

"Best buds since middle school."

"Are you hoping to attend MIT as well?" Vincenzo showed every sign of real interest.

"I wish. Mom and Dad made me apply. I didn't want to waste their application fee, but Dad especially just wouldn't listen. Even if I get scholarships, that's not happening. I'm not letting Mom and Dad go into major debt so I can attend an Ivy League school." The longing in Brian's voice said just how much he wanted to, though.

His parents were better off financially than Audrey, but they were still firmly in the middle-class income bracket and had four kids to put through college, not one.

"That seems to be a recurring theme." Vincenzo's tone was thoughtful.

"I'm planning to go to UMass Boston. We'll still be close enough to hang on weekends though, right?"

University of Massachusetts, Boston campus, was Toby's backup plan, too. It was a good school, but not the one Audrey knew either her brother or Brian most wanted to attend.

"Right," Audrey said, giving the teenager an encouraging smile.

She liked Brian. A lot. He'd been a good friend to Toby, even when her brother came out in high school and some of his friends dropped him because of it. Brian dated girls, but he'd joined the Gay-Straight alliance on campus to support his best friend.

Conversation around them settled down once the game started. Vincenzo's comments and loud team support showed that not only was he fully aware of which position Toby played, he had a genuine understanding of the game.

"I didn't realize you were such an enthusiastic fan," she said to him after a particularly loud shout of approval accompanied by him standing up to give it. "I thought Sicilians were all about European football."

"Soccer has never been my game. There is something very satisfying to the primitive in me to watch men face each other in such direct combat."

"It's a game, Enzu."

"Tell that to the young men doing their best to take your brother out at the knees."

"Don't remind me." Football was a dangerous sport, and

the wide receiver got tackled more often than the quarterback got sacked.

"He's fast and talented."

"He is."

"He is not interested in playing at university?"

"Maybe."

"But he is not looking for an athletic scholarship?"

"No." She did not want her brother's college education dependent on him being on the football team. "Football is a huge time commitment. Toby can handle it now, but MIT's courseload is terrifyingly heavy."

"Terrifying for him, or for you?" Vincenzo asked with too much insight.

"I just don't want him locked into playing sports when he might need that time to study."

"You're very protective."

"Someone has to be."

Vincenzo didn't reply, going back to watching the game. Very vocally.

When halftime came Audrey suggested getting something warm to drink. Vincenzo sent one of his security guys for hot chocolate, which was not what Audrey had meant. But it did give them the chance to take Franca behind the bleachers to run off some of the amazing amounts of energy stored in the body of a four-year-old.

When the game resumed Franca crawled into Audrey's lap. The third quarter was only half over when the small body went lax in sleep against her.

The look Vincenzo gave Audrey and the sleeping child was odd, almost tender. "Do you want me to take her?"

"No, she's fine. I can't believe she's sleeping through your cheering, though."

"Me neither. It must be a child thing."

"I remember my Danny at that age. He could sleep through an earthquake," a woman in front of them said.

"He did." Her husband turned his head to them and

winked. "We lived in California and he slept right through me carrying him to a doorway and holding him through the after-tremors."

Everyone laughed, but Audrey's heart squeezed. She wanted that. She wanted stories to tell when her children were teenagers; the shared experience of a lifetime spent with another person.

The prospect that Vincenzo might choose someone else for Franca and Angilu's mom grew more painful by the day. Her desire to be the one had never only been about Toby, but Audrey's desire to make a difference in the small children's lives had only been a vague concept before.

Now she knew them. Knew how much Angilu loved his bath time, how important it was to Franca to have her pictures hung on the walls of the nursery. The little girl had been ecstatic when Audrey had showed her a photo on her phone of Franca's latest floral masterpiece, hanging on the cubicle wall in Audrey's workspace.

It had taken less than the week they'd had together for both children to take firm footholds in Audrey's heart. She knew the days to come would only make her attachment to the children stronger.

The probability her heart was going to end up broken at the end of this only grew.

CHAPTER NINE

ENZU WAITED WITH Audrey outside the athletic building for her brother to come out of the locker room.

She'd tried to get rid of him, saying Franca needed to be taken home and put to bed.

Sending his daughter with one of the bodyguards to the limo took care of that particular argument. Enzu wanted to meet Toby, the young man Audrey had sacrificed so much to protect and raise.

"It could be another hour before he comes out." Audrey tried again.

He doubted it. Particularly after the offer Enzu had made to the team's head coach that afternoon. But he only said mildly, "You think so?"

He was not surprised in the least when a blond youth, easily as tall as Vincenzo, wearing jeans, T-shirt and letterman's jacket came bursting out of the door to the gym building. Eyes the same dark brown as Audrey's scanned the people milling around before landing on Enzu and Audrey.

Toby loped over, his blond hair dark with moisture. "Audrey!"

It said something about how agitated she was that his sister had not noticed the boy's exit until that moment.

She jumped, glared at Enzu and then turned to face her brother. "Hey, Tobe. Great game."

"It was," Enzu agreed with a nod, putting his hand out for the teen to shake. "Vincenzo Tomasi. You are a very talented ball-player, Toby."

The boy's handshake was firm and long enough to indicate confidence, but not so long he gave the impression of trying to prove anything. "Nice to meet you, Mr. Tomasi. Thank you for the party tonight. That's just sick."

"Sick means good in teenspeak," Audrey translated, before demanding, "*What* party?"

"Mr. Tomasi rented a bowling alley for the team and any friends we want to invite to celebrate our last game. Coach told us just now. Free games, shoe rental, food and soda until midnight."

Audrey gasped. "What? I didn't know—"

"Like I didn't know the guy you were dating was the freaking CEO of your whole company?" Toby interrupted.

"We haven't gone public with our association," Enzu inserted smoothly while Audrey looked like she'd swallowed her tongue.

"Why not?" the boy demanded brashly.

Enzu gave Toby a measuring look. "Because a man in my position does not announce who he is dating before he knows if that dating is going to lead somewhere at least somewhat long-term."

"I guess that makes sense." Toby didn't look entirely convinced, though. He turned to Audrey. "So, it's okay?"

"If you go to the party?" she clarified.

"Yeah."

"Yes, but I want you home by one."

"As to that," Enzu said before Toby could reply, "my country home is the same distance in the other direction as your apartment. I would like it very much if you came there instead."

"Why would I come there?" Toby asked in confusion.

"Because you and your sister will be spending the rest of the weekend with me and my children."

"What? You've got kids, man?"

"They're his niece and nephew," Audrey explained. "He got custody when his brother died six months ago."

"Oh." Toby's youthful features reflected honest sympathy. "I'm sorry, man. That blows."

"Yes, it does."

"Text me the address. I'll GPS it on my phone."

Audrey put up one hand in a gesture that meant stop. "Wait, I didn't agree to spend the weekend."

"Would you disappoint Franca and Angilu?" Enzu asked, knowing the answer. "They are looking forward to it."

"Angilu is a baby and you shouldn't have told Franca without asking me first."

"Have you not heard the saying *it is easier to ask for forgiveness than permission?*"

"Oh, how come I didn't know about *that* one?" Toby teased.

Audrey frowned at them both. "We don't have any clothes, pajamas, toiletries... No, it's impossible."

"I took the liberty of having everything necessary procured in your sizes. Including swimsuits. We have an indoor pool," Enzu said to entice the teenager.

Toby looked at Audrey as if to ask if Enzu was for real.

She nodded with clear resignation. "If he says he got us clothes and things, he did. And they probably cost more than I make in a month, too."

"But—"

"As your sister likes to remind me, I am a billionaire and my money can be used for more than making another business acquisition."

Toby looked flummoxed. "Get out of here. A billionaire. Nobody is a billionaire. Well, except maybe one guy I can think of."

So Audrey had told Toby *nothing* about Enzu. Interesting.

Regardless, Enzu found he liked the teen's attitude, so similar to his sister's. Toby treated the CEO of Tomasi Enterprises like any other person. It was refreshing.

"We do not all live in the media spotlight," Enzu said dryly.

"I guess, but, wow…that's just sick."

"I'm glad you think so."

Toby's face took on a serious cast. "We can go to your house, Mr. Tomasi, but my sister gets her own bedroom."

"Toby!" Audrey's cheeks washed a dark rose.

The boy looked at his sister. "Somebody has to watch out for you."

"You are absolutely right, Toby. I give you my word, your sister's room is all hers and not within two corridors of my own." He had his own suite in the mansion, near his niece's and nephew's rooms, but suitably distanced from those used for guests. It was Enzu's sacrosanct place to withdraw in privacy when family came to visit.

"That's okay, then."

"Oh, *is* it?" Audrey asked, voice dripping with sarcasm.

Toby set a direct stare on his sister. "Is he lying?"

"No, I'm sure he's not."

"You don't want to go to a house with a built-in pool?" Toby pushed.

Enzu had thought that would get to the teenager.

"I didn't say that."

"Audrey's not great when plans change unexpectedly," Toby said in an aside to Enzu.

Audrey snapped, "I like it even less when those changes are made on my behalf without my input."

"But I am getting that input now," Enzu argued.

Thinking about the unexpected visitor who had arrived that morning, Enzu was certain that Audrey would have more than his tendency to direct the lives of others to complain about before the end of the weekend.

"You could not have called me earlier?"

"No." She would only have said no.

"Preemptive strike, right?" Toby grinned. "We're studying game theory in relation to politics in my advanced government class."

Audrey sighed. "I give up. You…" She pointed at Toby. "Be at the mansion by one and not a minute later."

"Woot!" the boy yelled. "Thanks, Audrey. Thank you, Mr. Tomasi."

He hugged his sister and shook Enzu's hand enthusiastically again before running back toward the gym.

Audrey called out, "Toby!"

He stopped and turned around.

She jangled a set of keys. "The car is parked in the front lot."

He jogged back, grabbed the keys and then planted a kiss on his sister's cheek before thanking her again and leaving.

"He's got as much energy as Franca."

"More. He's still awake and will be for hours to come."

Enzu reached out and took Audrey's hand to lead her to the car. "You are not very angry, I hope?"

"More forewarned."

"Sì?"

"Oh, yes. I'm onto your tricks now, Enzu. You better watch out."

"I am shaking in my boots."

"You don't know how to shake, but I like the boots."

Inexplicably pleased, he smiled. "Thank you. My grandfather always said a man's shoes say a lot about him."

"Yours say you're willing to dress down for a football game, but your clothes are still worth more than my ten-year-old car."

"You need a new car, Audrey."

"No, I do not."

A ten-year-old car could not be reliable. "I am certain you do."

"Well, you aren't buying me one like you bought my

brother's team an after-game party. Thanks for that by the way."

"It was my pleasure." And, strangely enough, it had been.

Audrey shook her head, quiet until they reached the limousine. "No luxury sedan this time?" she asked. "Trying to impress me?"

"We needed room for Franca's carseat." His niece's seat was buckled securely in the safest spot in the limo, in case of an accident. The middle of the seat that backed up to the privacy window, which left the one facing it empty for Enzu and Audrey.

Audrey tilted her head, her delicate brows drawn in thought. "There would have been room in the sedan."

"I did not want to spend the ride home in front with the driver while you were in the back with her," Enzu explained.

Even if they'd taken one of the security SUVs it would have been the same. Unless Enzu drove, and for long distances his security team and insurance underwriters preferred he not do so.

Being CEO of such a successful company had limitations most would never even consider.

"That would be romantic if this wasn't part of an extended interview." Audrey gave him a cheeky grin as she settled into her seat.

He laughed. "But you know the truth."

"I do."

And the truth was he enjoyed every moment of the forty-five-minute drive, talking with Audrey in hushed tones, even though Franca had proved capable of sleeping through much louder noises.

Audrey might have been surprised a week ago when Enzu insisted on carrying Franca inside instead of leaving it to one of the bodyguards. But she'd spent a week witnessing this business genius's very real efforts to fulfill the role of parent.

Yes, he took some things for granted a man with less power, influence and money might not, but Enzu cared.

And Audrey found that genuine desire to be a good father an incredible turn-on. After spending six years in sexual limbo, it was disconcerting to find herself affected so strongly by pretty much *everything* this man did.

They were on the first riser of the grand staircase when a masculine voice spoke from behind them. "Who is this, Enzu?"

Enzu stopped and Audrey followed suit, before turning back to see who had spoken.

The dark-haired man with an insouciant air was unmistakably Vincenzo's father. He made it into the tabloids often enough to be readily recognizable even if Audrey hadn't done her research on the Tomasi family.

Enzu had been slower to turn around, but now he faced his father, who stood in the large foyer as if he belonged there. "Giovannu, this is Audrey Miller. Audrey— Giovannu Tomasi, my father."

"You can call me Papa, Enzu. Using my first name is your mother's affectation, not mine." The older man winked at Audrey. "My wife does not want anyone to know she is old enough to be Enzu's mother. And after all her plastic surgery not even I believe it."

"Don't be snide, Giovannu." Enzu looked down at Audrey. "You may join my father for a drink while I put Franca to bed, if you like."

"I'd prefer to help you with her." No way was he leaving her alone with this social shark downstairs.

The tightness around Enzu's mouth relaxed slightly. "As you wish."

"Surely it does not take two adults to put one child to bed?" Giovannu opined.

"I know you did not think it took either parent when you

were raising *your* children," Enzu said, in a tone that could have cut glass. "We will agree to disagree."

The older man winced and stepped backward, as if needing to create physical distance between them. "Whatever you say, son."

Enzu didn't reply.

He didn't speak again at all until after they had changed Franca into her pajamas and tucked her into bed. Mrs. Percy nodded her approval of their endeavors before disappearing silently into her room.

"Do you know she frightens me more than my old nanny used to do?" Enzu asked with a small smile as they traversed the long hall toward the curved stairway.

"She takes her job and the wellbeing of her charges very seriously."

"*Sì*, but even so she cannot replace a mama who loves them."

The absolute lack of doubt in Enzu's voice came from experience Audrey wasn't about to question. Besides, she agreed. "Oh, so now you admit that to *be loving*, a woman might actually need to love Franca and Angilu?"

"You may have a point in that regard."

"So, your parents are here to visit?" she asked, stopping before they began their descent of the stairs.

Enzu, appearing no more eager to rejoin his father, halted and leaned against the railing. "Giovannu only. My mother is ensconced in their Manhattan townhouse."

"Your parents live in New York City?"

"When they are in the country, yes. Or at least on this coast. They prefer five-star hotels when staying in LA."

"And your father is here without your mother because…?" Audrey prompted, knowing full well Enzu could shut her down at any moment.

"Giovannu ran out of money and reached the limit on his credit cards."

"I didn't know that was possible for a billionaire."

"*My father is no billionaire*. He has no income but the one from our family's bank."

Definitely a touchy subject.

"He wasn't interested in striking out on his own like you did?" she asked carefully.

Enzu gave a bitter laugh. "Not a chance. That would have required the willingness to work. His income from the bank's profits is only a few million a year, which he is required per their prenuptial agreement to split evenly with my mother."

"He's used up this year's dividends?" she guessed.

"And then some."

"So he's here to mooch?"

Enzu laughed, the sound harsh. "He would be severely offended to hear you say so."

"But he *is* looking for a loan?"

Enzu's blue gaze burned with emotions she doubted he realized were there and wouldn't be happy if he did. "I do not extend credit to my father, but he knows he is welcome to stay here."

"And maybe he wants to see you and his grandchildren," she offered gently.

"He wants to avoid my mother after his spectacular breakup with his latest mistress."

"Oh."

"*Sì.*" Enzu let out a frustrated breath. "My parents took no responsibility for their children and take even less for their own lives now."

"You support them?"

"Not directly. His shares at the bank provide Giovannu's income."

"But only because you keep the bank running in the black?"

"*Sì.*"

"You're a good man, Enzu."

He shook his head, but then he didn't see himself the

way she did. He was a driven businessman. No doubt about it. But Enzu was also an adult man who provided financially for his parents even though they never gave him a reason to do so.

He'd taken responsibility for his niece and nephew when other men in his position would have foisted them off on other family. He had an entire cache of cousins, aunts and uncles back in Sicily.

"Will your mother be showing up to cause your father difficulty?"

His weekend at the mansion was seeming less and less like a retreat and more like a war zone by the minute.

"It is a possibility," Enzu admitted.

"Really?" Audrey asked, not sure she wanted to deal with both of the older Tomasis.

"If he does not come crawling home, tail between his legs, soon enough for her you can count on it."

That didn't sound like imminent threat, though. Audrey let her tense shoulders droop in relief. "Will he? Go home, I mean?"

"Oh, *sì*. Frances has income from her parents as well as her half of the bank dividends. She can provide a much more entertaining lifestyle than he will experience here."

Man. Audrey had always known money was no panacea, but who said it was easy to be a billionaire with parents like that?

"Want to go for a swim?" she asked on sudden inspiration.

"My father is expecting us to share dinner."

"Are you hungry?" They'd had chili dogs at the game.

"Not particularly."

"You did buy me a swimsuit?"

Blue fire from his gaze licked over her body like she was already wearing it. "*Sì*. It is in your room."

"The one I'm not sharing with you," she teased.

"Your brother is very protective. It is clearly a family trait. I am impressed."

"We watch out for each other, but I have to admit his efforts to play *big* brother can be a little embarrassing."

"Oh? Have you experienced that very often?"

"Not ever before, actually."

Enzu laughed, the sound free of the bitterness that had been hanging over him like a cloud. "Let's go swimming, *biddùzza*. I find I am very keen to see you in swimwear."

"It had better be a one-piece," she warned.

His eyes taunted her. "And if it is not?"

"I'll wear a T-shirt over it."

"That T-shirt?" he asked, referring to the white one she wore under her bright pink sweater.

"Unless you had your personal shopper buy me another one?"

His lips tilted on one side in an enigmatic smile. "Fine."

"What do you know that I don't?"

"Nothing, I am sure."

"Innocent does not look believable on you."

There was that laugh again, and her heart warmed to hear it.

"Come, I will show you to your room and have Devon inform my father we will not be joining him for dinner."

She should feel guilty at the snub to the older man, but Audrey would do almost anything to dispel the pall that had come over Vincenzo after only talking to his father for a couple of short minutes.

The swimsuit turned out to be a bikini.

It wasn't scandalous. The bottoms covered Audrey's butt cheeks, the triangles of the top covered her breasts, and for that she was grateful. However, the smooth expanse of her belly was naked—as was her entire back. She wasn't comfortable with that much skin on display.

So she put the T-shirt on and then donned the bright white thick Turkish robe she'd found on the back of her *en-suite* bathroom's door. Whoever had bought her clothes had even provided a pair of spa shoes in her size.

Audrey slipped them on before leaving her room, only realizing that she didn't know which way to go for the pool when she was in the corridor.

Enzu pushed off from the wall opposite her door, where he'd been leaning and waiting. "I forgot to tell you the pool is on the basement level."

He wore a robe like hers, except his was embroidered with his initials and he had not tied it, revealing his olive-skinned, muscle-layered physique.

Heat flushed up her body, sending urgent electric messages to her core. Audrey had thought her reaction to him was bad before, but right now she just wanted to *jump* him.

Shoving extremely inappropriate thoughts deep into her psyche, she said, "I probably would have figured that out, but I'm glad you didn't make me go searching."

If her voice was a little breathy she could hardly be blamed. Not in the face of provocation like an only partially dressed Vincenzo Tomasi.

"The thought of you stumbling in on my father at his dinner while you are dressed or rather *undressed* as you are is enough to send chills down my spine."

"I'm perfectly covered." *Her robe was tied.*

"How long would you manage to keep that Turkish cotton around your body in his presence, I wonder?"

"You don't think he would try…?" No. Vincenzo could not have meant *that.* She for sure wasn't going to say it.

"Seduce you?" His lips twisted with distaste. "I would guarantee it."

Assuming Vincenzo knew his father best, she didn't deny the possibility. "Trust me, my robe would stay firmly tied."

"You think so? My father can be very charming."

"I may be ridiculously susceptible to you, Enzu, but I'm not usually a pushover with men."

"No, I don't suppose you are."

The fact she was a twenty-seven-year-old virgin did not need to be said out loud.

CHAPTER TEN

HER FIRST STEP into the basement paradise had Audrey gasping.

Located through a set of sliding glass doors opened with Vincenzo's palm print, the indoor tropical jungle was beyond magical.

Lush foliage flourished under a wall-to-wall ceiling of full-spectrum light panels. The air was warm and humid, but comfortably so. A path of mosaic tiles the colors of sand and earth wound through the tropical plants.

"This is incredible, Enzu," she breathed in awe.

"It is one of my favorite places to retreat."

"I can even hear birds."

"That is the sound system."

The fragrance of exotic flowers teased at her senses. "Don't tell me the flowers aren't real?"

"Most of the plant life is genuine."

It took her a moment to realize the area was untinged by the smell of bleach. "No chlorine in the pool?"

"Salt water and minerals."

The sound of rushing water reached her ears. "Is that a waterfall?"

"*Sì.*"

"May I see?"

He smiled, openly pleased by her response to his small

piece of paradise. "I will give you the full tour before we take advantage of the pool."

"I would love that."

The walk to the waterfall was short.

It cascaded over an outcropping of rocks, splashing into a pool that looked at first glance like a natural body of water. Closer inspection revealed the tiled walls and base done in colors to emulate the dark brown silt found in a lake. Muted lighting glowed along the bottom to make swimming safe.

Bamboo loungers covered with thick cushions the color of caramel sat to one side of the pool. One looked like it could be used as a double bed, it was so wide.

"Fantastic," Audrey breathed.

Vincenzo took her hand. "There is more."

He led her along the meandering path to a wild garden of hibiscus, orchids and lilies in vibrant colors. A dining set that complemented the loungers by the pool sat in the center.

Audrey could imagine both very romantic and relaxed family meals shared here. "It's idyllic."

"Sì."

"Would it be possible to have lunch down here tomorrow with the children? I think they would enjoy it." The baby's highchair could easily be brought down.

"That is an excellent idea, *biddùzza*. Speak to Devon and he will see to it." Vincenzo tugged on Audrey's hand. "Come. We are not finished with our tour."

What more could there be?

The *more* turned out to be a grotto, its manmade cave walls covered in moss, the ground around the small bubbling pool spongy with it as well. More flowers and abundant foliage grew to either side of the cave opening.

"It's a hot tub?" she asked, tempted to skip the swimming altogether when she saw it.

"Yes, but we keep the temperature at ninety-eight degrees now that the children make use of the pool room."

"Pool paradise, more like."

"Even workaholics have to have their indulgences."

She grinned, looking around at the amazing underground jungle. "This is some indulgence."

"Are you ready for our swim?" Vincenzo asked.

After a last longing look at the hot tub grotto, Audrey nodded. "You bet."

The path looped around to come out on the other side of the pool from where they'd begun.

Vincenzo pressed something on the bark of a tree trunk and a small panel popped open. One of the *not* natural plant life, then. A moment later the bright daylight turned to the gentle orange glow of sunset. The bird sounds grew quieter and were joined by soothing music.

He hung his robe on a hook she hadn't noticed. The sight of the billionaire in European swim trunks was not for the faint of heart. The snug, dark fabric accented his incredible body and did nothing to hide an enviable endowment.

Audrey could not look away. "You're beautiful," she blurted out and wasn't even embarrassed by the proclamation.

There was no shame in such an inescapable truth.

He laughed, the sound strained, his eyes darkened with desire. "Men are not beautiful, *amore*."

"A masterpiece is beautiful, whatever the art form."

"You would compare me to a work of art?"

"What else?"

"A flesh-and-blood man who will not make it to the pool if you do not stop looking at me like that."

"We're going swimming." That was the plan, right?

"Sì." He put his hand out. "Now, come here, *biddùzza*. You can hang your robe with mine."

She walked toward him, not conscious of telling her

legs to move, and stopped a foot away, but made no effort to remove the robe.

His hands dropped to the tied sash, olive skin dark against the white, even in the softened light. "May I?"

"Yes." It came out a mere whisper, but he heard.

"You have nothing to fear, Audrey. It is just a swim."

"Is it?" she wondered, not really asking him.

He tugged the belt loose so the robe parted to reveal her T-shirt and swimsuit-clad body. Delighted masculine laughter made her smile.

He pushed the robe off her shoulders. "You decided to wear it?"

"My T-shirt?"

"*Sì*, your cotton armor."

She shrugged. "I don't wear bikinis. I never did. Not even when I was a teenager."

Humor continued to glow in his gaze, like he had a joke he wasn't sharing, but he didn't say anything more as he dealt with the robe. Her gaze skimmed his body—she could not help it—and snagged on the growing bulge in Vincenzo's trunks.

Whatever amused him was also turning him on.

In an unexpected explosion of movement Vincenzo ran and dove into the pool, barely making a splash on entry.

His head broke the surface, dark hair slicked to his skull with water, rivulets of it running down his face, neck and broad shoulders. He grinned at her, his expression less guarded than she'd ever seen it. "Are you coming in, Audrey?"

"Not *biddùzza?*" she teased, moving closer to the side of the pool, one small step at a time.

"Always you are beautiful. No more so than you will be in the pool in your T-shirt, I think."

She did not know what he found so eternally funny about her top. "Is it warm enough?"

"It is a very comfortable ninety-two degrees."

Warm enough for the children to swim comfortably. "Too warm for laps?"

"The heating system is on a schedule. The temperature begins dropping at midnight and is cool enough for exercise at five-thirty in the morning. The heater goes to a higher temperature at eight and it's comfortable enough for play by lunchtime."

"That's nice."

His mouth curved in a knowing smile. "*Sì,* but it will be even nicer when you are *in* the water."

She nodded, but made no move to slide out of her spa shoes and join him.

"Audrey?"

"Uh-huh?"

"Are you coming in?"

"I want to."

"So…?"

"What am I doing here?" she asked him.

"Swimming?"

"I mean, why me…not one of the other candidates?"

"No more meaningful discussions, *amore,* not right now. We are going to *play.*"

She sighed. "Why do I think you don't mean Marco Polo?"

"We could play that if you like," he said, dark promise in his voice.

The image of Vincenzo reaching out to *find* Audrey after she called *Polo* burned into her brain. "Uh…maybe not."

"As you wish." But there was laughter lacing his tone.

And she liked that. Too much.

"Are there steps?" She looked around the pool and spied a handrail on the far side, near the waterfall, the top obscured by drooping vegetation.

Vincenzo moved toward the side where she stood and put his arms out in unmistakable invitation. "Jump, *amore,* I will catch you."

"I don't think that's a good idea." But she was slipping out of her shoes, wasn't she?

"You know you want to. You are not the cautious one."

No, she really wasn't. No matter how hard she tried to be "the responsible parent" for Toby's sake.

She jumped.

Vincenzo caught her with a carefree laugh that lodged in her heart, bringing their bodies together in the water.

She laid her hands on his wet shoulders, reveling in the feeling of powerful muscle beneath her fingers. "It *is* warm."

"I told you."

"You did."

"I will not lie to you, Audrey." His expression and tone said this wasn't part of the lighthearted play.

Or maybe it had not been play all along. Leaping into his arms had taken trust. Something Audrey did not easily extend to others. Not after her parents and Thad's betrayals.

"I know, Enzu."

"You trust too easily."

She laughed. "That just proves you can't read my mind. Believe me, I *don't*."

"Then I am honored."

"And I am wet."

"Sì." He looked down her body, the air around them suddenly, inexplicably crackling with sensual electricity. "Very much so. You are extremely tempting, *biddùzza.*"

"No more tempting than you." She didn't have to be experienced to know she wanted to do things with this man that did not include paddling through the water.

"I am very glad to hear you say so."

"Are you?"

"Sì. While my ardor is unmistakable and easy to see, I cannot be certain the tempting peaks of your nipples have drawn into tight buds from desire or the water."

"My...?" She glanced down between them and realized suddenly why he found her wearing the [...] so amusing.

Neither it nor the bikini top hid her tingling nipples, but the T-shirt itself didn't hide anything else, either.

"White fabric goes transparent in the water," he pointed out unnecessarily.

"I knew that."

"But you forgot?"

"I wasn't thinking."

"I take it you never entered a wet T-shirt contest at university?"

"No! Barnard wasn't co-ed." And she never would have entered such a thing with her no more than average curves anyway.

"There is no competition now, just a very alluring woman in an extremely provocative swimming costume."

"I didn't mean to make it provocative."

"I think that might be what makes it even more so. Your innocence, the hidden body no longer hidden, wet fabric that keeps me from feeling silken skin." His words were a husky whisper against her ear and ended with his tongue flicking out to tease her.

Chills of sensation washed over her from that tiny touch.

"Do you like that?" he asked in a hushed tone.

"I don't know."

"Let's give it another test, then." This time he teased the shell of her ear before tugging on her lobe with gentle teeth and then placing hot, wet kisses to the super-sensitive spot behind it.

She groaned. "I like it."

A small huff of laughter sent air across the sensitized skin and left goosebumps in its wake. "You are very responsive, *amore*."

"You are very practiced."

"No lover is exactly like another, believe me."

"You're trying to say it's different with me?" she asked in disbelief.

"*Sì.*"

She shook her head.

"Did we not just establish I would not lie to you?"

"But—"

"When I touch you, you are the only woman in my arms, the only one in my mind."

Her throat constricted with emotion and she could find no words to reply, so she did the one thing she knew that to this point she'd been good at.

She kissed him.

He allowed it for scant seconds before taking over the meshing of their mouths, claiming hers with his tongue. His taste melded with hers, creating an addictive flavor.

They moved through the water, but she could not be bothered to lift her head and see in what direction they went. She trusted her body to his care as she melted into the kiss.

Water receded against her skin, indicating that they were moving into the shallow end of the pool. And then he shifted and she felt a solid sloped surface against her back. The pool steps were flanked by foot-wide ramps that could be used for a steadying hand to enter the water and he must have laid her down on one.

He broke the kiss to lean up, away from her. "Let me have your T-shirt."

She didn't think about denying him. It wasn't as if the garment kept her modesty anyway. According to him, it was more exciting than if she'd simply left it off.

But he wanted it off now, and so did she. She craved the sensation of wet, naked skin against skin.

She took hold of her hem and began to peel the wet T-shirt from her body. He helped, his hands sliding against her skin. Whether by accident or design, she didn't care. Every little touch excited, making her need more.

ized suddenly why he found her wearing the white T-shirt so amusing.

Neither it nor the bikini top hid her tingling nipples, but the T-shirt itself didn't hide anything else, either.

"White fabric goes transparent in the water," he pointed out unnecessarily.

"I knew that."

"But you forgot?"

"I wasn't thinking."

"I take it you never entered a wet T-shirt contest at university?"

"No! Barnard wasn't co-ed." And she never would have entered such a thing with her no more than average curves anyway.

"There is no competition now, just a very alluring woman in an extremely provocative swimming costume."

"I didn't mean to make it provocative."

"I think that might be what makes it even more so. Your innocence, the hidden body no longer hidden, wet fabric that keeps me from feeling silken skin." His words were a husky whisper against her ear and ended with his tongue flicking out to tease her.

Chills of sensation washed over her from that tiny touch.

"Do you like that?" he asked in a hushed tone.

"I don't know."

"Let's give it another test, then." This time he teased the shell of her ear before tugging on her lobe with gentle teeth and then placing hot, wet kisses to the super-sensitive spot behind it.

She groaned. "I like it."

A small huff of laughter sent air across the sensitized skin and left goosebumps in its wake. "You are very responsive, *amore*."

"You are very practiced."

"No lover is exactly like another, believe me."

"You're trying to say it's different with me?" she asked in disbelief.

"*Sì.*"

She shook her head.

"Did we not just establish I would not lie to you?"

"But—"

"When I touch you, you are the only woman in my arms, the only one in my mind."

Her throat constricted with emotion and she could find no words to reply, so she did the one thing she knew that to this point she'd been good at.

She kissed him.

He allowed it for scant seconds before taking over the meshing of their mouths, claiming hers with his tongue. His taste melded with hers, creating an addictive flavor.

They moved through the water, but she could not be bothered to lift her head and see in what direction they went. She trusted her body to his care as she melted into the kiss.

Water receded against her skin, indicating that they were moving into the shallow end of the pool. And then he shifted and she felt a solid sloped surface against her back. The pool steps were flanked by foot-wide ramps that could be used for a steadying hand to enter the water and he must have laid her down on one.

He broke the kiss to lean up, away from her. "Let me have your T-shirt."

She didn't think about denying him. It wasn't as if the garment kept her modesty anyway. According to him, it was more exciting than if she'd simply left it off.

But he wanted it off now, and so did she. She craved the sensation of wet, naked skin against skin.

She took hold of her hem and began to peel the wet T-shirt from her body. He helped, his hands sliding against her skin. Whether by accident or design, she didn't care. Every little touch excited, making her need more.

He did something with her T-shirt and then put it down behind her.

"I want to touch you." His voice was thick with desire.

Unable to speak, she nodded.

His gaze burning into hers, he reached around behind her and undid the clasps on her bikini.

Her hands went of their own volition to her chest, holding the triangles of cloth in place. "What about your father? Will he come down here?"

"No."

"You're sure?"

"He does not have access."

"What about—?"

"*No one* will interrupt us."

"What if—?"

He placed one masculine finger against her lips. "Shhh. This is my sanctuary. No one will bother us, unless there is an emergency even Devon cannot handle."

"Is that your standing order for your time down here?"

"*Sì*, though I have a light on the access panel I can turn to green if I am merely looking to relax, not get away completely."

"It's not green right now."

"No, *amore*, it is most definitely red."

"Good." Mustering her courage, she let her hands fall away from her bikini top.

The wet fabric clung to her breasts.

Vincenzo's hands raised to hover a hair's breadth from touching. "May I?"

"Yes," she breathed.

He pulled the fabric away and tossed her top to the side of the pool, the blue fire of his gaze never breaking from hers. *"Molto bèdda."*

"You aren't looking." Air rushed over her wet skin, making her already tight nipples tingle and sending arrows of pleasures directly to her core.

"Aren't I?" he asked as his mouth drew closer to her own.

There was a message here, but she could not decipher it. Rather than trying to figure it out, she shifted her head so their lips met.

Vincenzo hummed in masculine approval as his arms came around her, his hands settling on her naked back. Her excited peaks brushed his hair-covered chest and she shivered in reaction to the cascade of sensation that caused.

He pressed their lips together more harshly than he'd ever done, his mouth possessive and insistent. The kiss was different than any they'd shared so far, and it required a response unlike any she'd given.

As demanding as the kiss was, there was also an element of seeking. Vincenzo wanted something from her and his sensual persistence indicated he was intent on getting it.

She didn't know what he needed. Permission? Sexual submission? The release of the reins she held so tightly on her own passion? For the first time in her life Audrey wanted to give him all of it.

Winding her arms around his neck, she melted into Vincenzo, determined to hold nothing back.

His growl of approval sent pleasure zinging through her. Trusting him completely in this, she didn't tense up as he tilted her back again.

Her nape settled against her T-shirt, her head comfortably held away from the hard slope she rested on. She vaguely realized in that small part of her brain still capable of logical thought that he'd rolled the wet cotton into a neck pillow.

The thoughtful provision for her comfort warmed her heart even as her body thrummed with sexual energy.

Vincenzo moved his mouth along her jaw, placing arousing kisses over her face and down her neck. Each caress of his lips felt like a brand, marking her as his.

A moment of chilling clarity washed over her. This

would change her forever. Vincenzo's lovemaking would ruin her for other men.

As if sensing the weight of her thoughts, he lifted his head, his handsome face set in stark lines of desire. "What is it, Audrey?"

No endearments. He wanted truth.

She couldn't have dissembled if she'd wanted to. "I won't be the same after tonight."

"No, *biddùzza,* you will not."

"No other man will touch me like you do." She didn't mean technique; she meant in her soul.

"No other men."

The harshness of his tone did not bother her. Though he didn't mean it as a long-term declaration, she still wallowed in the possessiveness of the words.

"There is only us."

"Yes," she agreed.

Without another word he lowered his head again, his tongue flicking out to trace her collarbone.

Audrey's entire body shuddered.

He slid his mouth down, kissing the top of her breast with suction that she knew would leave a mark. The thought of having proof of his touch on her body tomorrow made the flesh between her legs throb with pleasure and need.

The water lapped against her breasts, the waves caused by the movement of his body sending it over her nipples. Impossible to anticipate, each occasional caress of water over the highly sensitized flesh sent jolts of bliss through her.

Her hands scrabbled against the slick tile under her, but she couldn't find any purchase to ground herself.

Vincenzo leaned back, a dark smile curving his lips. "Will you trust me, Audrey?"

"I do." More than made sense.

The smile turned into something predatory, but there

was also an unexpected vulnerability in the depths of his blue eyes.

He took both her arms and pressed them over her head, wrapping his own fingers around hers so that one hand clasped her other wrist. "Keep them there."

Instead of anxiety, like she would have expected, peace settled over Audrey. Vincenzo expected nothing from her but her honest response to his touch. She did not have to wonder how to touch him, how to excite him.

His actions took the stress of her lack of experience away, leaving only desire behind. Unfettered by distress, her excitement broke over her in devastating waves.

He released her hands, clearly trusting her to keep them above her head. His fingers trailed down her arm and continued across her skin, leaving goosebumps of delight in their wake.

His hand stopped, fingers resting on her breast so lightly she shouldn't be able to feel them.

But the barely-there touch felt like each fingertip kissed her skin with fire, licks of pure sensation radiating around her aureole. He drew his fingers together, converging on her nipple.

A moan of pleasure snaked out of her throat.

"You are very sensitive to my touch." His fingers pressed more tightly on her peaked flesh, twisting gently. "I wonder how you will respond to my mouth."

Heat flushed her body at his words.

His head lowered tormentingly slowly toward her breast. Their gazes locked.

The sight of him touching her so intimately mixed with the physical sensation, increasing her pleasure nearly beyond what she could stand.

She arched toward him, but he laid his other hand on her stomach, gently pressing down. Audrey let her body relax.

Vincenzo smiled. "*Bene*. Good." His mouth finally covered her other nipple, his tongue flicking the tip before his teeth carefully worried it.

Audrey cried out, the sensation so intense it had to have an outlet.

His hand slid from her breast down her body until his fingertips rested against the top seam of her bikini bottoms. Vincenzo brushed his hand side to side, his fingertips slipping beneath the fabric.

"Enzu. Please…" She didn't know what exactly she was asking for.

Thad had touched her down there, but she'd never felt so desperate for *something*.

He lifted his head, catching her gaze. "You will trust me to take care of you."

"I will." She did.

Her body reverberated with need and something deep inside her told her he was the only one who could meet it.

His gaze warmed with approval that increased her desire as much as the touch of his hand on her body.

She licked her lips, tasting Vincenzo and the slightly salty water of the pool. He made a primitive sound of arousal and his mouth descended on hers, his kiss just as primal.

She responded with all of the sexual and emotional need surging through her, allowing him access, but using every technique of tongue-play she'd learned kissing this master of sensuality.

He touched her clitoris, a swipe and circle of his middle finger against swollen flesh that he repeated over and over again.

She squirmed, her body moving restlessly in the water, her thighs parting of their own volition, but somehow her hands never came down from above her head. Dark delight coiled inside her, tighter and tighter, until it was a compressed ball of energy in her womb. It sent little electric shocks directly to her core, making her most intimate place pulse.

She couldn't breathe, but she didn't want the kiss to end. Her heart was beating so fast she was getting lightheaded and she didn't care.

With a final swipe of his tongue, Vincenzo broke the kiss. He nuzzled her, placing open-mouthed kisses on her face.

His tongue drew a line up from first one temple to the corner of her eye and then the next.

"You cry with your pleasure," he whispered into her ear.

She didn't feel the tears, had none of the other indicators of crying, just drops of moisture leaking from her eyes. She hadn't even known they were there. "I'm sorry."

"No. You will not apologize for being so perfect. It is a rare woman who allows herself to feel so deeply when making love."

"How could anyone hold back from you?" Least of all a twenty-seven-year-old virgin.

"All that matters is that *you* do not."

"I can't."

"Then give your pleasure to me, *amore*. Come for me, now." The demand was whispered against her ear as a second finger joined the first against her clitoris, the double stimulation on either side of the bundle of nerves too much to deny.

She climaxed with a scream, her entire body arching against him, the sensual joy too intense too contain. He lightened his touch, but did not remove his fingers, pulling her through aftershocks that made her cry out and finally whimper with the surfeit of pleasure.

The whole time he whispered into her ear.

"*Bene.* Sweet Audrey, you did *so* well." And, as she floated on the euphoria following the cataclysm of her soul, "*Molto bèdda.* So very, very beautiful, my precious innocent."

She let her eyelids flutter closed, floating on a cloud of exultation, at peace in a way she had not been in all her adult life.

Vincenzo tugged her bikini bottoms off and Audrey let him without a murmur of protest. The sound of the wet fabric hitting the floor beside the pool told her he'd tossed the bottoms to join the top.

Strong arms slid under her back and knees and then water cascaded off her naked body as he lifted her from the water to rest against his solid chest.

His heartbeat was heavy and fast, his breathing rapid like he'd been for a run. Because he wasn't done yet. Not with her and not with his own pleasure.

A small secret smile curved her lips. *They were not done.*

He carried her to an extra-large lounger, laying her down on it before standing up.

She watched in sated expectation as he took off his trunks. His erection was dark with blood and so rigid the tip pointed upward.

Maybe it was her virgin sensibilities talking, but it looked like he had a loaded cannon between his legs. Thick and long, ready for action. The sight of him naked stole what was left of her breath.

Lassitude left her as excitement began thrumming through her blood again.

CHAPTER ELEVEN

"You're big." She licked her lips, the tiniest flicker of worry lighting inside her. "Maybe I should have had my first time with someone less impressive."

"No," he growled out, his expression going from lustful to saturnine.

Oh, he did not like that idea. Not one bit.

"I didn't." She pointed out the obvious.

His jaw hardened, a slight tick indicating her comment had not tamed the savage beast. At all.

"You gave me your trust?"

"Yes."

"You will trust me not to hurt you?"

"First times hurt, Enzu." She wouldn't let him make a promise he could not keep.

"There are ways to mitigate that pain."

"A lot of experience dealing with a woman's virginity, have you?" she asked, irritation pricking the haze of pleasure in a way her anxiety had not.

"None, in fact."

"Then how would you know?"

"Really? *You* must ask this?"

Once again she felt he was laughing at something she did not understand.

"Yes, I must."

"Research."

"No regrets?"

She almost asked him again how he could possibly doubt that, but stopped herself. He wanted a direct answer. No chance for any misunderstanding between them. "None."

"Bene." He began to draw lines down her body with his fingertips. "I am going to touch you."

"Okay."

He smiled. "Close your eyes and feel, *amore.*"

She did and he touched her. *Everywhere.* Alternating between soft skimming caresses and pressure that massaged muscles she hadn't realized were sore in her post-orgasmic bliss, he mapped every centimeter of her skin.

From the top of her head, which he massaged with adept, masculine fingers, making her moan in pleasure, to her toes, which he sucked one by one, sending carnal delight zinging up her legs directly to that place in between, to all spots in between, Vincenzo claimed her body with his fingers, lips and tongue.

She was vibrating with the need to climax again when he was done. The leaking tip of his sex said he was feeling the same ache for completion, but he did not move between her legs.

Instead he lay back, his blue gaze holding hers hostage. "Do you want to touch me?"

"Yes." Even more than she wanted that ultimate pleasure.

"You have ten minutes. You may touch me anywhere, any way you like." He waited a beat. "But you cannot make me come."

She nodded her understanding, reaching out immediately to caress his chest. She didn't worry that she should start somewhere else. He wanted her hands on his body and that was all that mattered.

He'd taken the pressure off needing to bring him to climax by ordering her not to do so. And he'd shown her that every inch of skin could be an erogenous zone.

All she had to do was follow her own desires and he would like it. She wasn't sure how she knew that, but it was an absolute certainty within her.

Maybe she was just too close to the edge sexually to stress about knowing *how* to do this right, but her lack of practical experience simply didn't matter right then.

She traced the lines of his face, letting her fingertips trail down his neck. "You are so handsome."

"Thank you, *bèdda*."

She shook her head. How could he thank her for the truth? She used her whole hands on his chest, rubbing her palms over the small brown disks with tiny hardened nubs in the center before mapping each line of his six-pack.

If she let herself touch his arousal she wouldn't touch anything else, so she skipped his pelvic area altogether and moved down his legs. She wanted to see if she could bring goosebumps to his flesh like he'd done with hers.

His olive skin did not pimple with sensation, but he shivered for her, his muscles jumping. She was pretty sure she was close to time when she bent over his weeping erection and licked the moisture drops right from the tip.

That got her a groan and the restless shifting of his hips.

She laved his entire shaft, returning again and again to the sweet, nearly clear fluid welling in his slit. She bathed him with her tongue, taking in his intimate flavor, breathing deeply of the male musk emanating from the heated skin.

She was so lost in her own pleasure at tasting him she did not register the hand gently pushing her head.

Not toward the masculine treasure, but away. "Your time is up, my Audrey."

She lifted her head, her eyes unfocused so that he was a blur for the seconds it took her pupils to contract. "Another time I want unlimited minutes to taste and touch you."

"Not tonight."

She inclined her head in agreement. She'd promised him her trust tonight. That she would follow his lead.

"Come here." He put his arms out in invitation.

She didn't hesitate, but dove for that embrace, her body landing on top of his. She kept her legs together, the disparity in their heights making his truly impressive erection settle in the seam of her thighs, just brushing the apex.

"You are delightfully sensual," he praised as he traced her lips with his fingertip.

"I'm not like this with anyone else." Never had been with Thad, and no other man had tempted her out of her self-imposed isolation into anything like this.

"Then it is a precious gift I will treasure."

The reminder that this was a test-drive for the job of his convenient wife flickered through her mind, but passion smothered it.

He rolled them, one strong thigh pressing hers apart.

Was it time? She was ready. More than ready. All trepidation at what was to come was drowned in the waves of bliss being touched by and touching him sent crashing through her body.

She allowed her body to soften under him, spreading her thighs to ease his access.

He leaned up, his hand reaching down to her moist intimate flesh and one finger slipping inside her very slick channel.

"You are very wet, *biddùzza*." There was a wealth of satisfaction in his voice.

She just hummed her pleasure at the very intimate touch.

He spread the wetness up over her swollen clitoris until all of the sensitized flesh between her thighs was slippery with the inescapable proof of her pleasure.

He shifted his body, adjusting their positions so the bulbous tip of his erection sat against her clitoris. Then he pressed down with his pelvis and thrust upward, causing his entire length to drag against her slick folds and pleasure center.

"What...? This isn't..." She couldn't finish a thought, not with him stimulating her most sensitive spot the way he was.

"This is exactly what I wish to do right now. I will make it very good for you. *Sì, amore?*"

"Yes." There could be no other answer.

He continued thrusting until she met him, movement for movement, pressing upward, the ball of pleasure building and centering inside her and then just hovering there, on the edge of bliss as he continued the maddening frottage.

"Please, Enzu! I need..." she begged, her body supplicating along with her words.

He thrust three more times, each glide of his hardened flesh against hers slower and conversely more powerful than the last.

Then he reared back, his hand going down, two fingers sliding inside her without warning, pressing deep.

She winced, her body jerking when they hit the barrier inside, but she told him, "Don't stop."

"I will not."

He massaged her inside, pressing inexorably against the thin membrane that protected her sexual innocence. His other hand slid up her thigh and he cupped her mound protectively. "Mine."

She nodded, her throat too tight and dry to speak.

He pressed his thumb against her clitoris, drawing tight circles over her aching nub.

Suddenly the pleasure inside her was acute, the climax that had hovered so close but just out of reach on the verge of exploding. Her body went rigid, every muscle contracting in anticipation of pleasure so big it would have frightened her with anyone else.

"Now, my Audrey. Come for me again," he instructed as his fingers thrust deep inside her.

Ecstasy detonated and fireworks went off inside her, making her womb contract and every nerve-ending in her body explode. This time she screamed so loud and long her throat was raw with it.

His fingers pressed through the barrier of her body. The pain was there, but unable to break through the astonishing pleasure for dominance of her senses.

He had taken her virginity, but kept his promise. Vincenzo had not lost control, his beautiful sex had not breached her body, stretching her and tearing through the fragile membrane with inevitable pain.

He knelt there, between her legs, and took himself in hand. Once, twice and then his face twisted in a rictus of ultimate delight while he ejaculated onto her body.

When he was done, he used the same hand he'd touched himself with to rub his seed into her skin like lotion. The look in his Mediterranean-blue eyes made the act one of primal claim-staking she was not even sure actual intercourse could have rivaled.

For tonight Audrey Miller belonged wholly to Vincenzo Tomasi. Full-stop.

They cuddled together in the warm humid air and she slid into a doze. Not sleeping deeply, but not fully alert, either. Tonight had been nothing like she could have ever expected or even dreamed about.

Maybe Toby had been right. Maybe Vincenzo was a superhero. He was certainly more man than any other she knew.

He woke her from dreams born of memories they'd made only that night with a kiss. "We must shower and return to our rooms to dress. Your brother will be arriving in less than hour."

Nothing else would have convinced her it was a good idea to leave the security of Vincenzo's arms. But at his words she forced herself to sit up, drawing away from him.

She shivered at the cold not touching him sent through her soul, despite their balmy environment.

He seemed to understand, putting his hand out to take hers. "Come, we will shower together."

She wasn't about to argue at the continued opportunity for closeness.

He led her to a shower tucked into an artfully arranged group of oversize leafy green plants between the pool and the grotto with the hot tub.

The hot water felt wonderful on muscles that were not used to the rictus of extended and multiple orgasms. Even more soothing were Vincenzo's hands as they lathered and washed her body, gentle between her legs as he rinsed away the smears of blood left behind by her torn barrier. He let her wash him as well, his semi-erect manhood growing into full hardness even though it had not been her intention to turn him on.

He laughed when she apologized. "Do not worry about it, *biddùzza*. We will arrange a night when I can lose myself in your body until we both pass out from exhaustion."

She gasped, a zing of desire sparking through her in response to his promise.

They donned their robes after they dried off, but Vincenzo tossed both of their suits with the used towels into a laundry bin.

He held her hand as they made their way in companionable silence along the path back to the sliding glass doors.

A happy yowl sounded, before two balls of fur streaked across the path only to collide into one mass of rolling, spotted fur.

Audrey yelped, but Vincenzo merely laughed. "Finally they decide to show themselves."

"What in the world are they?" she asked, her heart still lodged somewhere in her throat.

Vincenzo grinned, his expression more open and relaxed than she'd ever seen it. "They are ocicats—a feline similar in coloring to the ocelot, but smaller and fully domesticated."

"You have pets?" she asked in absolute shock.

"They were both damaged when their breeder's facility was broken into."

"Damaged? In what way?"

"I will show you." Vincenzo whistled like he would to a dog.

Strangely enough the cats stopped their play and came trotting over. One had only three legs; the other had an ear that had been torn and had healed with ragged edges.

Audrey dropped to her knees and put her hands out for the animals. "You poor lovelies. What are your names, hmm?"

"Spot lost his leg to a glass shard. It was either amputate or lose the cat. Rover's ear was either the result of his brethren's stress at the break-in or more glass. The breeders didn't know which."

"How awful. Dog's names, though?" she asked with teasing disbelief.

"Devon insisted." Vincenzo's lips twitched. "The ocicat is known for acting more canine than feline."

"Your majordomo found them?"

"He learned the breeders planned to euthanize them. Spot and Rover cannot be shown competitively and therefore could not be sold for the usual exorbitant rate. They had already been spayed in preparation for transferring ownership, so there was no hope of using them to breed."

"That's terrible."

"Devon agreed."

"You must have, too, to take on pets."

Vincenzo shrugged.

"They live down here?" she asked.

"They will not leave, though they have been given many opportunities to roam the rest of the house. They suffer a version of agoraphobia. The animal psychologist believes it is the result of their trauma during the break-in."

"You took them to an animal psychologist?" she asked, giving up the fight against loving this complicated man to bits.

If there had ever been a question that he would own her heart completely, there wasn't one any longer. She was head over heels.

"Devon had the psychologist come here."

Audrey laughed as she straightened, having made friends with the two ocicats. "Of course he did."

No wonder Vincenzo didn't keep any birds down here. Even a contained aviary wouldn't be safe against these two. "Are the cats the reason you don't allow your family down here?"

"It is not my entire family. Only my parents."

"Why keep this place from them?" Vincenzo gave so much to his family, even if he didn't recognize that fact. "That just seems so out of character for you."

The look he gave her was hooded. "Do not begin to think you know all that I am. At the most basic, I am ruthless and determined to have my own way."

"What does that have to do with your parents coming down here?"

"My mother would insist the temperature, which is perfectly modulated for the plant life, be changed, that the air be dehumidified. My father would use this place as a way to impress his playthings."

"He would bring his other women here? To your *home*?" Never mind just to the jungle paradise. That was sick—and not in the good way.

"His opportunistic gene is highly developed."

"You make me happier and happier that we opted out of dinner with your father."

Vincenzo nodded, but then sighed. "If you become a

permanent part of mine and the children's lives you will have to learn to deal with my parents."

That tiny little *if* hurt in ways she didn't have the emotional stamina to examine right then. "Are the cats safe with the children?" Audrey asked, needing to focus on something other than that two-letter word.

"Spot and Rover are as affectionate as puppies. Devon informs me that both children adore them, though Angilu cannot chase them down like Franca."

"Devon informs you? *You* have never brought the children down here?"

Burnished color streaked Vincenzo's sharp cheekbones. "No."

"Why not?"

"I did not know how." Vincenzo's jaw locked, his tall body going rigid with tension.

The admission had not come easily.

"Enzu, even brilliant billionaire tycoons are not born with an instant manual on how to be a parent."

"I had practice."

"How?"

"Pinu. He was ten years younger than me. Frances and Giovannu had no interest in parenting. His nanny was not a *warm* person. I held him when he cried, fed him, played with him, taught him what I knew of family and life."

"You were a good brother." No wonder Vincenzo was so determined to offer Franca and Angilu something more.

Again with the shrug. "But the world looks very different from the eyes of a thirty-six-year-old man than that of a ten-year-old boy. What I felt qualified to do as a child is more daunting than any business venture as an adult."

She reached up to brush a hand along his jaw and brought her other hand up to his cheek. The familiar touch drew their surroundings in until it was just the two of them. "You are doing fine, Enzu. Franca and Angilu are thriving."

"Now they are."

"You cannot change what their life was like with their parents."

"No, I cannot." Pain laced his tone and guilt she did not understand dulled his gorgeous blue eyes.

"Enzu, give yourself a break. Do you have any idea how incredible it is that you turned out so responsible and caring, considering the way you were raised?" Considering just how badly he'd done in the parent gene pool.

He jerked his head away from her, moving back, the openness and relaxation from just moments ago completely gone. "Do not be fooled, Audrey. I do not deserve either accolade."

"How can you say that?"

"I knew. I knew and I did nothing about it."

"What did you know?"

"How like our parents Pinu had become, and still I left Franca in his care."

"She was *his* child."

"But at the very least I could have been a more involved part of her life."

Audrey could not argue that reality, but it wasn't right for Vincenzo to take it all on himself, either. "You trusted your brother to follow your example, not that of your parents."

"Why should I have been so blind? He followed their example in every other way." Vincenzo shook his head, self-disgust lacing every word. "Franca barely knew me when she became my child six months ago. I had only seen Angilu once, right after his birth."

She could have argued that Vincenzo had been busy earning a living for his entire family, his brother included, but Audrey thought it was more than that. "Maybe you stayed away because you couldn't stand to see the truth of how your brother had turned out."

"I am not a child, to hide from the truth."

"You're also not perfect, Enzu. No one is."

"I have no excuse."

"But you do have reasons and you're doing your best to make it right."

"Now that you are here I am making headway."

"What do you mean?"

"I have gotten to know the children more since you have come into their lives than I did in the first six months they lived in my home."

Well, that was because they hadn't actually lived with him. But she didn't say so. She had a feeling Vincenzo would just make that another guilt implement to flog himself with.

"Come. We cannot change the past and talking it to death is of benefit to no one."

"Enzu—"

"Your brother will be here soon," Vincenzo interrupted her. "Do you wish to meet him in your robe, with your hair a tangled mess on your head?"

"No. Definitely not."

"Then we had best hurry."

He did not take her hand again as they left the pool paradise.

CHAPTER TWELVE

TOBY WAS RIGHT on time.

Audrey barely managed to get her hair brushed into a neat if wet ponytail and to put pajamas on under the robe before he arrived. He teased her about using the pool without him, but was easily placated by the promise they would be indulging the next day.

Toby and the children thoroughly enjoyed their afternoon in the pool paradise. Toby was as impressed by the indoor jungle as Audrey, and he fell in love with the ocicats, but he really shone with Franca and Angilu.

The baby adored the water and decided Toby was his favorite playmate in it.

Vincenzo emulated some of Toby's play with Angilu and seemed surprised but very happy when the baby responded just as well to him. All three of them had a blast together while Audrey and Franca worked on the little girl's ability to float.

Both children were going to have to have age-appropriate swimming lessons if they were going to live even part-time in a house with a pool. They might not have access to the pool room, but children got into places no one thought they could.

Or so the parenting books Audrey had read suggested.

They didn't see Giovannu Tomasi until dinner that evening.

"I do not understand why we are having dinner practically in the afternoon," he complained to Vincenzo.

"It is six-thirty in the evening, hardly the afternoon. I have explained my dinner hour has been shifted to accommodate the children, so we can eat together as a family before their early bedtime."

That had been one of Audrey's suggestions and it made her happy he'd taken it and was clearly so protective of the change in his schedule.

Giovannu frowned. "That can hardly be convenient with your business schedule."

"I make it work," Vincenzo said with thinning patience.

"You cannot neglect your business responsibilities in order to play happy families, Enzu."

Vincenzo grimaced and Audrey wanted to smack his father upside the head. "If you are very concerned, I am sure Enzu would appreciate you taking a more active role in running the bank," she said.

"As his most recent and hardly his last *lady-friend,* you are hardly in a position to have an opinion on the subject, Miss Miller," Giovannu said with a double dose of condescension.

Toby made a sound like steam escaping a boiling kettle, but Audrey shook her head at him. In a very real sense, Giovannu had a point.

"On the contrary. In our time together, Audrey has proved to have a better understanding of myself and my business than you have ever been capable of, Giovannu."

The ice in Vincenzo's tone would have frozen Audrey where she sat if it had been directed at her.

Giovannu simply waved his hand, as if dismissing Vincenzo's words. "I have a vested interest in the continued success of the bank and your company."

Vincenzo sat very erect, the blue gaze he directed at his father glacial. "First, let me be very clear, you have zero interest in *my* company. Neither you nor Frances will benefit financially, now or ever, from Tomasi Enterprises. Second, Audrey is absolutely right. If you are so worried about Tomasi Commercial Bank I will be happy to cede the presidency to you and you can run it into the ground for all I care."

Vincenzo gave his father a chilling star.

"But do not think I will step back in to bail you out. It *will not* happen. Third, you will treat any guest I have invited to my table with the utmost respect, or you will lose the privilege of being a guest in my home at all. Do we understand each other?"

Giovannu stood up, his expression one of affronted pride. "Perhaps it is time I returned to my own home. I expect better treatment from my son than this."

Vincenzo simply inclined his head. "Devon will arrange for someone to help you pack."

His son's agreement clearly shocked the older man. His mouth opened in slack-jawed disbelief.

It occurred to Audrey in that moment that Vincenzo had probably never stood up to his father like this. He'd made it clear that for the most part he practiced a live-and-let-live-with-an-allowance policy toward his parents.

Vincenzo was driven by his obligation and care toward his family. It would take a great deal to force him to show this ruthless side to those he felt responsible for.

She couldn't help the way it touched her heart he was defending her role so mercilessly.

Audrey looked around the table to see how the children and Toby were taking this altercation.

While Franca sent worried glances toward the men, plainly aware of the tension between them, the actual meaning of their discussion had gone over the child's head. She continued to eat her dinner while having a quiet conversation with Percy about the merits of fresh carrots with dip over the cooked ones on her plate.

Toby was busy playing with the baby, ignoring the argument to the point he'd deliberately turned his back toward Giovannu.

Audrey bit back a smile at her brother's silent message of disgust for the older man. She shifted her attention back to Vincenzo. His eyes were on her. His father was standing silent dumbfounded to his right.

She winked at Vincenzo. He jerked back as if startled, but then a smile started at his mouth and spread like sunrise to his oh-so-compelling blue eyes.

"That won't be necessary. There is no point in allowing a little tiff to drive a wedge between father and son," Giovannu said, as if he and Vincenzo were still engaged in active discussion. "However, I do think I will have my dinner later. This early epicurean hour does not agree with me."

Vincenzo just shrugged, his gaze never leaving Audrey. "If that is your wish."

"Yes, well…" Realizing no one was going to ask him to stay, Giovannu left.

Toby sent Vincenzo a look of understanding. "No offence, but I think your dad and mine went to the same school for jerkwads."

Vincenzo's bark of amusement exploded into full-blown laughter and soon the whole room was laughing. Even the baby and Franca, though the confusion on her tiny face said she didn't know *why* she was laughing.

Audrey, however, gasped out Toby's name in admonishment. "Language!" she prompted.

He grinned and nodded, but the look he shared with Vincenzo said neither male was particularly repentant.

She'd just arrived at her desk on Wednesday morning when Audrey's mobile made the sound of keys on a typewriter, indicating she had a text message.

Smiling, she grabbed the phone, and a small laugh fell from her lips as she read what it said.

R U packed? No PJs needed.

She hadn't seen Vincenzo since Sunday night, but he'd been texting her. Early morning "wake-up" messages right after her alarm went off. Quick reminders to eat, or take her breaks.

Apparently Vincenzo and Toby were texting buddies now, too, and Audrey's brother had ratted her out about skipping breakfast with her new early hours.

Vincenzo was a lot more fluent in textspeak than Audrey and sometimes she spent more time deciphering his messages than answering them.

She sent him pictures of Franca and Angilu from her afternoon visits with them. She shared little jokes about her day and was ridiculously pleased when he started doing the same with her.

The sexy texts had started Monday night, right around bedtime. One-word reminders of their time together on Saturday. Oblique promises of what was to come over the holiday.

Vincenzo had invited her and Toby to stay the four-day Thanksgiving weekend with him and the children at the mansion. Amazingly, the workaholic billionaire was taking almost the entire time off.

Hence his packed schedule leading up to it.

Audrey curled in the chair beside the window in her guestroom.

She was reading. Not watching for the arrival of Vincenzo's car in the drive below. Not.

Percy had arrived with the children in the afternoon. Audrey and Toby had driven up after she got off work. If she'd been thinking, she would have put off their arrival until the following morning.

But Toby had been so excited to return to the mansion and Vincenzo's indoor pool, not to mention the state-of-the-art workout facility. And maybe Audrey had hoped she would get to see Vincenzo.

He was supposed to arrive sometime tonight, after a video conference with one of his West Coast subsidiaries.

She'd had some vague idea about waiting up for him downstairs, until they had arrived and discovered that Giovannu Tomasi was still in residence. Not that he had joined her and the children for supper.

Giovannu had, however, asked Audrey to keep him company while he ate. Since she'd already helped Percy put Franca and Angilu to bed, Audrey had not had a ready excuse for turning him down. Mindful of what Vincenzo had said in regard to learning to deal with his parents, Audrey had realized she shouldn't make up one, either.

It had not been a pleasant hour, but Audrey had not walked away bleeding, either. Giovannu had begun by pouring on the charm, apparently genuinely under the impression that he was utterly irresistible to the opposite sex.

She'd shut him down in a way guaranteed to get her point across: by pretending not to even notice the flirting and responding to him as if he was a particularly trying older uncle.

She'd dropped unsubtle hints that she considered him too old to be seen in *that way*. And wasn't he lucky to have a wife of so many years? After all, many men of his advanced years faced a lack of companionship.

As she'd thought they would, her comments had fallen on the fertile ground of the true egoist's latent insecurities.

She'd looked into his break with his last mistress and discovered that the gossips were convinced the much younger woman had dropped him cold for a younger man with a less impressive financial portfolio.

Giovannu had shifted his approach in what Audrey had come to realize was an attempt to eject her from Vincenzo's life, even if she did not understand *why*.

She'd ignored the barbs, insinuations and blatant accusations that she was an unsophisticated nobody who had no place with a man like Vincenzo. Audrey had had twenty-one years of experience dealing with superior attitudes and verbal put-downs before her parents had cut her from their lives.

Giovannu Tomasi was merely a more spoiled example of the breed with a deeper sense of entitlement. Even if she hadn't known her relationship with Vincenzo was based on his plan to provide a loving mother to Franca and Angilu, Audrey would not have given Giovannu Tomasi the satisfaction of letting him get to her.

Infuriated by her unconcerned reaction, he had quit the field.

Audrey had thought she might take a swim to relax before bed, but had discovered quickly that the memories the jungle paradise evoked when she did not have the distraction of the children were going to be anything but calming.

It would have been different if Toby had joined her, but he'd taken his swim earlier and was indulging in a late-evening workout in Vincenzo's gym.

So Audrey had returned to her room, determined to read until she was settled enough to sleep. Now it had hit midnight and she'd read the same paragraph at least a dozen times before giving up on her book. So she simply sat.

Not waiting.

But definitely in no shape to sleep, either.

The sound of an approaching helicopter arrived scant seconds before its lights swept the front of the mansion as it headed to the helipad in the back.

Audrey surged to her feet. *Vincenzo had arrived.*

Uncaring that she wore only her favorite masculine-style black and white striped silk pajamas, she rushed for the door of her bedroom. She grabbed the matching black robe just before she exited the room.

Tugging it on and tying the sash haphazardly, she hurried down the corridor. She realized she'd left her slippers behind when her bare feet slapped against the cold marble of the staircase.

It was only as she reached the bottom of the steps that it occurred to Audrey she had no idea where to go from here.

"If I may, Miss Miller?" the majordomo spoke from Audrey's right.

"Oh, Devon. I'm so glad you're here. I thought I'd meet Mr. Tomasi, but…" She let her voice trail off with a shrug.

"Is he expecting you?"

"Um…no."

"I see."

"You do?"

The majordomo nodded. "You have no plans to meet Mr. Enzu, however, it is likely he is aware of your impulsive nature and may well be expecting you."

Audrey didn't even blush. Much. "Right."

"Come this way." Devon led her to a smaller, more warmly decorated version of the formal living room. "It is Mr. Enzu's habit to indulge in a single-malt whiskey in here before retiring to his suite when he arrives after the dinner hour."

"I'll wait for him here, then."

"That would be best," Devon said with a significant look to her unslippered feet.

Audrey's toes curled instinctively into the rich pile of the carpet. "Yes, well, um…"

Devon didn't seem to expect her to finish her thought as he lit the gas fireplace and poured a finger of amber liquid into a rock glass before placing it on a table by the chair nearest the fire.

"Would you like a nightcap?" he asked her.

"No, thank you." She'd had wine earlier and wasn't much of a drinker.

Devon inclined his head in acknowledgement. "I will leave you, then."

Audrey sat in the wingback chair nearest the door, her

feet tucked under her. The minutes dragged and she wondered if Vincenzo would forgo his drink tonight. Perhaps Devon hadn't thought to tell him she was waiting?

The sound of two masculine voices in tense conversation approached the opened door.

"I am very sorry to have to tell you, Enzu. But you must believe me. You are my son, after all. I care about you," Giovannu was saying, his smarmy voice doing a remarkable job of sounding sincere. "She made a pass at me."

"Did she?" Vincenzo asked, his tone so void of emotion Audrey had no clue what he was thinking.

Who had made a pass at that old letch? One of the maids? Audrey couldn't believe it. Devon wouldn't hire someone so lacking in taste.

"It was very upsetting, Enzu. There's a wild side to that little Miss Butter-Wouldn't-Melt-In-Her-Mouth. I'm ashamed to say I was tempted, Enzu. You know my weakness for aggressive younger women." He sounded ashamed, and so *concerned*.

Audrey wanted to puke. She had no doubts that, whatever poor female Giovannu was talking about, *she* hadn't been the aggressive one.

"Audrey tried to seduce you?" Enzu asked in that same dispassionate tone.

"No!" Audrey said forcefully at the same time Vincenzo's father claimed an affirmative.

That disgusting, deceitful *toad*.

She jumped up from the chair and stormed to the doorway, noting the expressions on both men's faces. Giovannu's showed shock before he quickly masked it with that fake troubled caring.

Vincenzo's gorgeous face showed no more emotion than his voice, his blue eyes entirely shuttered.

"You've got an amazing poker face," she told him.

The facade cracked with the tiniest fissure of barely-there amusement. "Do I?"

"What are you doing here? Dressed like that?" Giovannu indicated her PJs as if Audrey had come downstairs in a see-through negligee. "Do you see what I mean, Enzu? She couldn't have known you would be home. She was lying in wait for me."

Audrey stomped up to the older Tomasi and glared. "You are an ass." She crossed her arms over her chest. "And what's more you're an idiot if you don't think your son knows it."

"How dare you?" Giovannu drew himself up. "I am a Tomasi. You are nothing. A nobody."

"In that you are very wrong, Giovannu." Vincenzo gently pressed Audrey back so he stood between her and his father still in the hallway. "Audrey is my guest and I warned you what would happen if you disrespected my *invited* guests."

"Didn't you hear me? She tried to—"

"Seduce you?" Vincenzo laughed, the sound cold as the Arctic. "I do not think so."

"You are calling me a liar?" his father demanded in what sounded like genuine outrage. "You would take her word over mine?"

"In a heartbeat." Vincenzo lifted his phone to his ear, pressing a button. "Devon, arrange to have Giovannu's things packed. He will be leaving within the hour."

"What? You cannot kick me out of your house, Enzu. You are my son!"

"Keep saying it. Someday I might believe it means something to you." Vincenzo sounded tired.

"Of course it does. Your mother and I care about you. We care about our grandchildren."

"So much that you couldn't be bothered to even check in on Franca or Angilu once since they arrived this afternoon."

"*She* told you that!" Giovannu glared daggers at Audrey.

"Mrs. Percy told me." Vincenzo shook his head, an ex-

pression of disgust coming over his features. "Do you honestly believe I would put two innocent children in your
care?"

What was he talking about? Giovannu didn't want to
take care of his grandchildren. That was patently obvious.

"*If* I believed I could not do an adequate job of raising
them," Vincenzo continued, "I would sooner put them in
the care of our family in Sicily. You will never take control of Franca and Angilu, or the shares in the bank Pinu
left them."

"Enzu—"

"Don't try to deny your plans. I've had my investigator looking into things. You and Frances have decided you
want control of Pinu's wealth and you used the breakup of
your latest affair to show up on my doorstep."

The disgust in Vincenzo's tone was mirrored in his expression.

"Only you're such a rotten parent model you didn't even
know how to ingratiate yourself as potential caregivers.
Let me give you a hint. Being on the outs with your wife
over an extramarital affair and ignoring your grandchildren completely isn't even in the ballpark."

Audrey understood then. To Giovannu, the children
were no more than the key to accessing more money for
his profligate lifestyle.

"I am severely offended you would accuse me of wanting to take the children in some effort to control their in-
heritance. They deserve two parents, not one workaholic
uncle who understands making money and nothing of the
human condition."

And that explained why the man wanted Audrey gone.
The argument held no water if Vincenzo was paying attention to the children, and in Giovannu's mind that was
only happening because Audrey was around.

Vincenzo shook his head. "Coming from anyone else,

...rds might hurt. From you? They are nothing more ...the braying of the ass Audrey called you."

Giovannu made as if to come into the room, but Vincenzo blocked his entry. "Your things and your car will be leaving my property in…" he looked down at his watch. "…fifty-four minutes. If you do not leave with them, you will be walking, but you *will* leave."

Then Vincenzo shut the door on his astonished father before making a beeline for the drink Devon had poured. He tossed it back like a shot.

Audrey winced in sympathy for his throat and nasal passages. Expensive whiskey like that was not meant for shots.

"Do you want another?" she asked, though.

He shook his head and turned to face her. "You waited up for me."

"I wanted to see you."

"Was there something particular you needed?" he asked, in what she'd come to think of as his business voice.

"At the risk of providing fodder for your father's fantasies of my *aggressive sexual behavior,* I was sort of hoping for a kiss good-night."

"Is that *all* you were hoping for, *biddùzza?*"

"Tonight?" She nodded. "Tomorrow is Thanksgiving and I have to be up early to cook."

"I do have a chef on staff."

"Yes, but he doesn't know how to make Toby's favorite sweet potato pecan pie. And I'm not giving up my recipe for stuffing, so that means I make it."

"You are serious about this? You are not teasing me?"

Audrey shook her head. "Some things have to be done out of love. Holiday food is one of them."

"So, stuffing and pie?"

"And maybe a green-bean almond casserole. Danny's mom loves it."

"So they agreed to come for dinner?"

"Yes. Thanks for inviting them." When Toby had told

Vincenzo that he and Audrey had a tradition of shar~~~~
Thanksgiving with Danny's family, her billionaire had insisted they be included in tomorrow's festivities as well.

"Danny will be staying the rest of the weekend, too. According to Toby, both boys are *'totally psyched.'*"

"Toby told his friend about the indoor pool?"

"And your gym. Apparently it's *sick*." She grinned.

"I am glad it passes the teenager test of worthiness."

Audrey walked over to Vincenzo and laid her hand on
his arm. "I'm sorry about your dad."

"You have nothing to apologize for."

"You never believed him for a moment. About me making a pass at him."

"Even if I had not known how little regard you have for
my father after last weekend's visit, I am in the premier
position to judge the likelihood of you behaving aggres-
sively sexually."

"Yes? I think I could become aggressive with you."

"That is good to know."

"Is it?"

"Si."

"What about the control thing?"

Suddenly it was his hands on her arms, and she was
standing so close she could feel Vincenzo's heat.

"What *about* the control thing?" he asked in that darkly
seductive voice she'd heard so much of on Saturday night.

She tilted her head back, her lips parting as she tried
to think of what to say, but she could not remember what
they were talking about.

His kiss was full of promise, heated desire and *restraint*.
Vincenzo ended it much too quickly. "Any more of that
and you won't be leaving my bed until Thanksgiving dinner tomorrow."

She nodded and then shook her head, seriously discom-
bobulated.

He laughed softly, the frustration of dealing with his

father no longer etched so deeply into his expression. "I will walk you to your room." He kissed her again, outside her door, and then smiled down at her. "I like your pajamas, by the way."

"They're not sexy."

"Define sexy."

"You know."

"I do know. You have me hard and seriously tempted to ignore your need to rise early to show your love for your family through cooking. Definitely sexy."

She was smiling when she closed her door with Vincenzo on the other side.

CHAPTER THIRTEEN

VINCENZO HAD NEVER experienced a family Thanksgiving dinner like the one Audrey orchestrated.

He'd worked this holiday and pretty much every other one each year since taking his first job at the bank. The American branch of the Tomasi family did not *do* traditional holidays.

He'd had to take a call from Europe early that morning, but the rest of the day was clear and Enzu enjoyed it. Audrey and Toby's friends were a warm and boisterous family, the love between parents and children obvious and genuine.

They were all relaxing in the living room now that they'd eaten their feast. Danny's youngest sister and Audrey were playing with Lego on the floor with Franca. The teen's mother cradled a sleeping Angilu in her arms while the remaining children and their father played Monopoly.

Enzu didn't even know he had board games, but Devon had brought a stack of them on Audrey's request.

"She's a natural mom," Toby said as he sidled up to Enzu. "Audrey's got a nurturing streak as wide as the Grand Canyon and just as deep."

"Sì?" As if Enzu did not know.

It was one of the things he found most intriguing about Audrey Miller. She was so completely different than any woman of his acquaintance. Even Gloria, while an estimable PAA, could not be accused of being remotely family-centric.

"It's how I knew…" Toby let his voice trail off.

But Enzu thought he knew what the teen meant. "That you could go to her when your parents failed so spectacularly at their job of caring for you?"

"Yes." Toby's shoulders drooped and then he made a conscious effort to straighten them. "You know, I never looked at it as a failure on their part."

"Audrey didn't fail you, but they did."

"You're right. It cost her so much, though."

Vincenzo thought that was something Audrey would never count. "She's made it clear to me that she considers the cost worth it."

Toby shook his head. "I was just a kid, you know? I kept thinking they were going to change their mind and everything was going to be okay again."

"It was a reasonable expectation."

"Was it?" Toby asked.

"Audrey's actions should tell you how reasonable. She is a very good stick by which to measure sincere family behavior."

"She is, isn't she? I never want her to think her sacrifice has been wasted."

"It has not and I know she agrees with me."

"I'm just glad she's found you."

Vincenzo felt an odd sensation in the region of his heart. "Why?"

"I may not be going to MIT, like we dreamed, but I am going away to college." Toby had a very adult, very Audrey-like expression on his youthful face. "I didn't want to leave her alone."

"No?"

"She doesn't know it, but I applied to universities in New York, too. I've been accepted."

"I thought you and your friend planned to go to school in Massachusetts?"

"Not if it means leaving her on her own."

"You are a good man, Toby."

"Thanks. I think you are, too, Mr. Tomasi."

"Enzu."

"You sure? Audrey drilled polite behavior into me even more strictly than Mom and Dad used to."

"*Sì*. One day soon we may be brothers."

"You think?" Toby asked, excitement barely contained in his tone.

"I do, but you will not say anything to Audrey."

Vincenzo's decision was made, but he felt completely alien nerves about informing her of that fact.

"My lips are zipped." Toby made a zipping and locking gesture across his closed mouth.

Enzu grinned. "Good man."

Later that night, after the children were in bed and the extra dinner guests had left for home, Enzu surveyed the scene he had set with a critical eye.

Everything was ready for the final seduction of a very sensual virgin. Except one thing.

There were too many shadows cast by the clusters of candles on the tables on either side of his bed and the large chest of drawers against the wall. Enzu wanted to see more than their flickering radiance would afford when making love to his *biddùzza*.

He turned on the recessed ceiling lighting, adjusting it to a muted glow.

Better.

Audrey wouldn't even realize the luminescence from the multiple small flames had been augmented.

Casting a final glance at the king-sized bed piled high with pillows and covered with fresh crimson rose petals over the royal-blue silk sheet, he went to answer the soft knock on his suite's door.

Audrey stood on the other side, wearing her pajamas and robe from the night before. Her chocolate gaze reflected unmistakable trepidation and anticipation.

"You remembered slippers tonight," he said by way of a greeting as he stood back to allow her entrance to his personal sanctum, this one even more off-limits to others than his jungle paradise.

She nodded, making no move to come inside.

"Are you having second thoughts?"

Audrey shook her head, her lovely brown hair rippling and sliding against her robe.

He reached out and guided her inside, lust spiking in his belly from the simple touch of his hand against her silk-clad shoulder. She didn't balk but came without hesitation, despite her clear inability to take this step of her own volition.

Just as it had in the pool last week, her instinctual compliance intoxicated him more than the champagne waiting in the other room ever could. She gave herself so beautifully and completely to his desires. She ensnared him with bonds he could not hope to break.

And in her innocence she had no idea.

"I would like you to leave your slippers, robe and pajama bottoms here." He waited to see if she would comply, his atavistic instincts certain of her reaction even as logic insisted the connection between the two of them could not be that deep and elemental.

Against all rational expectation of her reaction, his words seemed to relax her as an undeniable air of tension surrounding Audrey bled away.

She toed off the ballet-style black slippers, managing to place them neatly to the side of the rose petals creating a path from his door, through the suite to the bed in the other room. She surprised him by removing the bottoms first, folding them and dropping them on top of the slippers.

When she went to untie her robe he reached out and gently took over the task without any previous plan to do so.

That lack of fore-planning should bother him. He *always* planned every action in the bedroom. His *control thing,* as Audrey called it, didn't just extend to his partners. Enzu demanded total restraint of himself.

Since his very first foray into sex Enzu had never once lost his self-mastery. Until the previous Saturday night, when he had kissed without thought and come within inches of burying himself inside Audrey's untried body.

It had been his knowledge that to do so would cause her unnecessary pain that stopped him, not his own willpower or plan.

"Enzu?" Audrey looked up at him with inquiry, but no mockery.

He'd lost himself in his thoughts and she was not amused by it, did not tease him about losing *control* of the situation.

"You are a very good match for me, *più amato.*" The endearment slipped out, but he would not take it back. *Best beloved.*

He also had no intention of telling her what it meant if she asked.

She didn't, only observed, "Not on paper."

"Externals are not important Not here. Not between us."

"You don't think so?"

"No."

"We are almost polar opposites."

He slid her robe from her shoulders and then dropped it over the back of a nearby armchair. "Perhaps that is what we both need."

"Yes." She smiled, a mischievous light shining in her brown eyes. "I don't think you'd find it nearly as much fun with someone as bossy as you are."

He chuckled, but cupped her cheeks, making sure their gazes met and she could read the sincerity and challenge in his. "I do not believe you would enjoy yourself as much with an overl.. ..ilized partner, either."

".. .. even sure I would have ever been open to an- ...r sexual partner," she admitted painfully.

"You have not been tempted in the past six years?"

She shook her head. "At first I was too hurt by the betrayal of the most important men in my life to trust anyone else enough to even go on a date."

"You were busy trying to keep a home together for you and Toby while finishing your schooling as well."

"Yes, but..." She swallowed, trying to turn her head from his gentle hold.

He would not let her. He sensed there was something important here he needed to know. "But what?"

"If I'd been open to it, I could have dated."

"You weren't." She'd already said so. "What is it you think is so important you need to hide it from me?"

Her eyes widened as if his insight shocked her. He almost laughed. Did she not realize he expended more effort reading her than he did his strongest business rival?

He thought back over their words, looking for a clue to what Audrey was trying to keep from him. "You said *at first.*"

Fear skittered across her expression.

"What came next?" Had she had a bad experience?

"Toby started high school and he did really well, academically, socially—he was well-adjusted all around."

"And he needed you less?"

"Yes, so I thought I should maybe start dating."

His gut clenched. "What happened?"

"I saw you."

It was so far from what he'd expected to hear Enzu dropped his hold on her face. "What?"

"You were visiting the bank. I saw you in the hall." Clear discomfort colored her voice. "You turned to say something to Gloria and I saw your face full-on."

"There is a portrait of me in the lobby of the bank building." She had to have seen his face before that.

"Yes. I'd looked at it a lot. Only not really consciously, you know?"

"No, I do not know."

"No, I don't suppose you would." She turned away and went to one of the huge bouquets of crimson and white roses that he'd had flown in to fill his suite.

"Audrey..." he prompted, his tone letting her know he would not drop this.

She reached out and ran a fingertip over one velvet blossom before leaning over to inhale the fragrance of the perfectly open blooms.

Her action wasn't necessary. The heady perfume permeated the suite from sitting room to bathroom and the bedroom in between.

She was stalling.

"What did catching a glimpse of your employer have to do with your dating?" he asked, thinking a more specific question would get her talking again.

She turned back to face him, the picture she made in the silky pajama top that just brushed her upper thighs nearly making him forget their conversation all together.

"I didn't see my employer in that moment."

"That makes no sense." Even when she'd worked at the bank, as its president Enzu had ultimately been her employer.

"I saw a man."

Not for the first time in this woman's presence, Enzu found himself speechless.

"A man I wanted."

"That was four years ago."

"Yes."

"So you did not date in hopes of one day catching my eye?" he asked in disbelief.

"No. I *never* thought I'd come under your notice. But it didn't matter."

"Why not?"

"I *couldn't* generate interest in other men."

"Even though you knew there was no chance you would have me?"

"It was so stupid, and I was determined to break the pattern once Toby had gone away to university."

As illogical as it might be, Enzu did not like hearing that. "You were going to date?"

"I'd even created a profile on one of those online dating sites."

"That needs to be taken down immediately."

"I deleted it before it ever went public."

"Good." He did not examine the relief he felt at that assurance. "So, what you are saying is that you've had a *celebrity* crush on me for four years."

"You'd think so, wouldn't you?"

"What else could it be?"

"Love."

"What? You cannot love someone you do not know."

"No, you can't be in love with a stranger. But the spark of love can be ignited. You've fanned it into a raging flame since that first day in your office."

He crossed to her, putting both hands on her shoulders, his urge to kiss her strong. "You are saying that you love me?"

"Yes. Isn't it stupid?"

"I have no experience with the emotion, but I do not think it is *stupid*, no."

"You don't?"

"No." Perhaps these feelings she had for him explained how stunningly she gave herself to him.

"You don't mind?"

"That you love me?"

"Or that when I came to you the first time I obviously had ulterior motives for approaching you?"

"If not for Toby, would you have approached me otherwise?"

"No."

"Then your motives were as you described them. Your attraction to me made it possible to act on your desire to help your brother."

"And Franca and Angilu. I thought I could make a difference for them, too."

He nodded, believing that all too easily now he had gotten to know her.

Giving in to the urge that would not go away, he brushed Audrey's lips with his own, knowing he could not afford to deepen the kiss yet. "We are done with this, *si?*"

Her eyes widened with distress. "With making love?"

"With talking." He shrugged off his own robe, letting it drop into a pile at his feet and giving Audrey an unblocked view of his arousal. "We have plans for tonight."

"You're very attached to your plans," she teased, but her voice was breathy and her gaze kept getting snagged on his erection.

"I am." Putting action to the sentiment, he led her back to the path of rose petals. "Come, we have many hours of pleasure ahead of us."

She licked her lips and then smiled. "No early morning tomorrow?"

"No." Mrs. Percy had already been warned not to expect him or Audrey to come for the children before lunchtime.

With the new game console Enzu had purchased for the game room, the teens had plenty to keep them occupied as well.

Enzu tugged Audrey along, the rose petals beneath their feet velvety soft against the deep plush pile of his suite's wall-to-wall carpeting.

Audrey gasped when they came into the bedroom.

He stopped and let her take in her surroundings before asking, "You like?"

"Very much. It's so...so romantic."

"A woman's first time comes only once."

"Yes, but..."

"You will never forget this night." He mentally shrugged off the arrogance he heard in his own tone.

She looked at him as if he'd lost his mind. "It could have happened in a broom closet and I wouldn't be able to forget it."

"Because you love me?" he found himself asking, when he'd had no intention of doing any such thing.

He clamped his jaw on any further unplanned verbalizations.

"And because you are my first." She didn't deny the love thing.

He poured them each a glass of champagne and handed Audrey hers before offering his glass for a toast.

"To first times."

The crystal clinked quietly, and then they both took a sip.

Audrey's eyes slid shut and she hummed before taking another sip. "This is very good."

"It is an excellent vintage from the South of France."

She laughed softly as her eyes met his again. "Of course."

"I thought a glass of wine would help your nerves." And if they were going to imbibe it would be something worth drinking.

"I'm not nervous."

The honesty of that statement was obvious in the sincerity of her tone, but also the relaxed lines of her body.

"Your trust in me is humbling." And very little made him feel that way.

"It feels right."

"Giving yourself to me?"

"Yes."

Because she loved him.

He let her take another sip of her champagne before removing her glass from unresisting fingers and placing both flutes, still partially full, back on the small table beside the bed.

"After tonight there is no going back. You understand this?" Their futures would be set.

For the first time anxiety flickered in her chocolate gaze. "Yes."

"Bene."

His kiss was intentional and deep.

Melting into him, she opened to his questing tongue without even a token resistance. Pleasure coursed through him. This woman was so perfectly matched to him sexually.

He would show her how right she was to trust him with her body so completely.

He let the kiss build until the need to touch her had become acute. What many did not understand in the type of lovemaking that excited Enzu the most was that he got as much satisfaction out of challenging his own control as that of his partner.

But the time to move things to the next step had come.

He allowed himself to caress her body through the silk of her pajama top, mapping her body's curves—the indent of her shoulderblades, the dip of her waist, the smooth outline of her hips, the soft expanse of her stomach, the gentle ridge of her ribcage, the pillowy curves of her breasts. He cupped them, squeezing and releasing until she made a restless movement with her hips.

Enzu moved on to tease her beaded nipples, sliding his fingers over the silky fabric covering them. He pinched them lightly, enjoying the way her pajama top encouraged his skin to slide off, and then repeating the maddeningly short touch again and again.

She moaned against his lips, the sound as exciting as if she had taken his rigid sex into her hand.

He ended the kiss, once again cupping her cheeks and forcing total focus between them. "I am going to take off your top now."

"Yes," she breathed.

He let his eyes warm with approval as he undid the first and second buttons in quick succession, caressing her breasts with the backs of his hands. The satin fell open to reveal smooth, creamy skin.

He leaned down and pressed sensual kisses to each gentle curve of her upper breasts. Letting his tongue flick out, he tasted the silken skin.

She gasped. *"Enzu."*

He undid another button, widening the gap in the fabric. It caught on the hard peaks and he let it stay there, teasing them both with her almost-nudity.

He dropped to his knees and nuzzled the fabric aside so he could take one raspberry bud into his mouth. Suckling, he teased the tip with his tongue while he skimmed his hands up the backs of her thighs to cup her naked buttocks.

Her hands landed on his shoulders, fingernails digging in hard enough that he knew he would have crescent-shaped marks there tomorrow.

"Please, Enzu, don't tease. I need you."

He lifted his head, giving her his most wicked smile. "You have only begun to need."

She shook her head. "No. You don't understand. I've wanted you so long."

"And you will have me, sweet Audrey. But in my time."

He waited until he saw acceptance in her expression. Willing her to remain still with his eyes, he finished taking her top off. It necessitated removing her hands from his shoulders, but he gave up one pleasure for the promise of a greater one.

She stood silent, still, completely exposed before him.

He had never been so turned on, and if he was not careful he would climax before he ever got inside her.

In an explosion of movement that made her cry out in surprise, he surged up and then lifted her into his arms. Showing her trust in him, she did not scramble to hold onto his neck, though both hands touched his chest, fingers splayed as if she sought to maximize the connection.

He laid her against the pile of pillows, stopping to enjoy the way the royal-blue silk set off her milky skin. Her hair fanned out over the pillow under her head in enticing disarray.

"Molto bèdda," he praised.

"The view's not bad from here, either." She smiled up at him, eyes half-mast with sensual appreciation.

She did not resist when he guided her hands to grip the iron bars of his specially designed headboard, stretching her body and arching her back so her breasts were on tempting display.

With careful hands he arranged her legs so they were spread wide and bent at the knees, pillows placed strategically for her ease.

"Are you comfortable?" he asked, his throat tight with intense desire.

She was blushing like the innocent she was, but she nodded.

"Words, *biddùzza*. I need actual words."

"Yes, I'm comfortable."

"Bene. If you become uncomfortable you can move, or ask me to move you."

"Ask you to move me?" she inquired in a tone laced with confusion.

"There is great pleasure in leaving the responsibility of every element of your comfort and pleasure up to me, *amore*."

"It doesn't seem fair."

"If it is my own preference it is a fair exchange. Trust

for trustworthiness. Ceded control for beneficial restraint. Pleasure for equal pleasure."

"Yes," she breathed out.

As he knew she would.

Goosebumps were forming on his skin at how well they fit. If he'd believed in such things, he would have thought they were connected on a soul-deep level.

"Thank you," he said, breaking his own rule of not saying the words for something that felt so right.

Her expression said she remembered that injunction from Saturday, but she didn't remind him of it. And for the second time in less than a minute he experienced profound gratitude toward the woman in his bed.

This time he was able to hold back the words, though. He leaned to the side and reached out so he could tug a silver tray with four porcelain dipping bowls within easy reach.

"What's that?" she asked.

"I have two weaknesses," he admitted, instead of giving a direct answer.

"I didn't know you had any."

"*Sì*. Even a control freak like me has his vices."

"I bet you have more than two of those."

He was impressed she'd immediately recognized that the two were not mutually inclusive. Not all vices became weaknesses. And he did not consider one of his weaknesses a vice. Audrey was simply Audrey, a woman like no other.

"I won't take that bet."

Her gaze flicked to the tray and then back to him. "What are your weaknesses?"

"These dipping pots are filled with four different kinds of chocolate." Again he forbore from giving her a direct answer, but he was confident she would figure it out.

"You're a chocoholic." The laughter in her tone and merry eyes did not actually spill out.

"I am."

"Good to know."

"Is it?"

"I think so."

"I am going to indulge, but there is one catch."

"Yes?"

"I will indulge myself…and you…so long as you do not move from your current position. Once you move, whether it is letting go of the headboard or shifting your legs, I will know the time has come to press forward in tonight's activities."

"So, I can squirm? I just can't break position?" she asked, to clarify.

"Precisely." Did she understand the rest of what he'd said as well?

"You're giving me the power to decide when we stop playing."

"Mmm…" he said in approval.

"I get to say when the foreplay ends?" she asked, like she couldn't quite believe it.

"*Si*, but when you are making that decision be aware you are cutting off one kind of pleasure, delight that can lead to many wonderful things, in order to pursue another."

CHAPTER FOURTEEN

"You're a fiend." She did not sound like she was making a complaint.

He laughed, his amusement tinged with harsh desire. She would never know how close he'd come to forgetting the game and going straight to the copulating.

But she deserved to be seduced, not merely taken. No matter how much they would both enjoy the joining of their bodies when it came.

He dipped his finger in the milk chocolate and then painted her lips with it, grateful she'd washed away her makeup before coming to his room.

"It smells yummy."

"It will taste even better." He leaned down and gave her a chaste kiss, transferring the chocolate to his lips as well.

Then he deepened the kiss, licking chocolate from her and inviting her with his tongue to do the same to him. The kiss lasted until every bit of chocolate was gone and he was wallowing in a flavor that was pure Audrey.

Forcing himself not to get lost in sensation, he withdrew to dip his finger in the white chocolate this time. He painted her nipples, covered the aureoles completely.

He put his fingertip against her slightly parted lips. "Do you want to taste?"

In answer, she opened her mouth and took his finger

in, licking and sucking with a natural sensuality that sent more desire raging through him.

Lowering his head, he showed her he could play that game, too. First he gave each breast a tongue bath, knowing the soft caress would be enough to tantalize, but not enough to satisfy.

She moaned around his finger, the sound part frustration, part pleasure. That was when he set about suckling the rest of the sweetness from her already tasty nipples. When they were clean of the candy he nibbled each nipple in turn, worrying them with his teeth as Audrey started to squirm, her sounds growing increasingly desperate.

He continued to paint her body with the different flavors of chocolate, letting her taste each one, either from his finger or his lips.

She seemed to like the dark chocolate the best, so he used it on her inner thigh, moving steadily closer and closer to her private, enticing musk.

He didn't put any chocolate on her sex before he tasted it. Her feminine essence needed no enhancement to be entirely alluring. He laved her lips and then pressed his tongue inside her, loving the way her entire body went rigid at this most intimate of kisses.

He moved up so that he could tease her clitoris with his tongue, pressing two fingers inside her and curling upward to stimulate her G-spot.

She gave a strangled scream, pressing her pelvis upward and her clitoris harder against the rigid tip of his tongue.

"Enzu, if you don't stop, I'm going to…" She didn't finish the thought.

But he had no trouble understanding what she meant. Did she think her warning was an incentive to actually withdraw?

He already knew she was close because her clitoris had gotten swollen and shifted infinitesimally upward, indicating her body's primal sexual reaction to his ministrations.

Knowing the time had come, he reached up with his free hand to pinch her nipple and roll it between his thumb and forefinger.

She screamed, climaxing with a whole-body convulsion, her inner walls contracting around his fingers, moisture gushing forth to make her so silky-wet he knew he was going to slide into her like melted butter.

He kept licking, but softened his tongue so her pleasure was prolonged, but not amped to the point of pain.

Suddenly her hands came down and pulled on him. "Inside me. Please, I need you inside me, Enzu."

He reared up, triumphant and so very pleased with his *più amato*.

For the first time in his life he resented the need for a condom, but that did not stop him from putting one on.

"Sunday night."

"What?" he asked, with no idea what she meant.

"We can go without a condom Sunday night. I inserted a vaginal ring on Monday afternoon. The information on the ring said we only had to wait seven days for the birth control be effective."

Just the thought of making love to her without a condom almost had him exploding. He didn't bring up the usual tests that should be done before allowing unprotected sex. He knew she was free of anything because she'd never been with anyone else, and Enzu had not had sex since his last physical with blood tests and an all-clear.

"I will eagerly look forward to Sunday night." Even if he had to fly with her back to the city Monday morning in the helicopter and send the others back by car on Sunday night, she would be in his bed.

Placing the head of his erection against her hot, tight and extremely slick opening, he waited for that addictive gaze to meet his.

"Do it," she pleaded.

He pushed inside, going slow, but not stopping. She

stretched around him, her body flushing with the effort of taking him inside her completely.

He took his time with the first few thrusts, spreading her body's natural lubrication until the drag of her body against his sex was not quite so tight.

Calling on a lifetime of self-control, he proceeded to make love to her with long, slow strokes until it was obvious from the way her body moved beneath him and the sounds she was making that she was building back toward another climax.

He pressed first one and then her other leg straight, making her even tighter, making it possible with an adjustment of his hips and swiveling his pelvis on each downward thrust to stimulate her clitoris.

"Oh! Enzu, yes…that's…I can't…"

Her incoherent ramblings drove his lust to heights he'd never experienced and soon he was slamming in and out of her, his mouth claiming hers in a kiss that told her everything about what he was feeling.

If she was listening.

His balls drew tight and he knew he was going to come very soon. He broke the kiss and moved his mouth to her ear to demand, "Come with me, *più amato*. Now."

He swelled, going hard as steel, and then white-hot ecstasy exploded out of him. She turned her head, catching his lips in a desperate kiss as her body convulsed, her second orgasm ripping through them both.

She went completely boneless beneath him, her eyes shuttering closed. "Amazing," she slurred.

"*Sì*. Unlike anything else."

She nodded drunkenly and he smiled, though he barely had the strength to pull out of her and roll to his side. He would deal with the condom in a moment.

She reached out and he met her questing hand with his, lacing their fingers. His concept of life and himself was in a shambles around him, shattered by lovemaking that for the first time in his life had actually been that.

The prospect of having to admit that truth to himself, much less aloud to Audrey, made Enzu break out in a cold sweat right there in his thoroughly debauched bed.

Audrey lay awake in Enzu's arms in the early hours of the morning.

It was more than a month since their first time together, but Enzu had not officially told her she was his *chosen candidate*.

He hadn't mentioned any of the other candidates since before he'd blown her mind that first time in the pool, though. In fact, he hadn't mentioned the whole looking-for-a-wife-slash-mother-for-his-children thing since Thanksgiving.

She wasn't sure how she felt about that. Their lovemaking was hotter than an active volcano, even the times they didn't play any of his control games.

She didn't want to give that side of their lovemaking up, but she liked knowing it wasn't necessary for intense sexual satisfaction. That they could have completely tender sessions that culminated in a pleasure so profound it was a spiritual experience, not just physical and emotional.

She hadn't known sex could be like that, but then she hadn't known it could be so fun and kinky, either.

No, the sex definitely wasn't the problem. There *was* a problem, though. While Enzu and she continued to spend time together with the children daily, they spent almost no time alone that wasn't dedicated to sex.

He shut down any conversation that might actually lead to talking about feelings. And that worried her. Because her feelings just grew stronger and stronger.

She couldn't imagine he was even considering marrying anyone else, but why hadn't he made it official? Was he waiting for Christmas? Did he have plans to propose under the tree Christmas morning, or something?

Enzu did love his plans, but she almost laughed out loud at the idea regardless. She didn't think he had that kind of romance in him.

So, what was he waiting for?

"What has you thinking so hard, *biddùzza?*"

"How can you tell I'm thinking?"

"Your body is not lax as in sleep. You are not initiating sex, or talking. So…thinking."

She looked up at his beloved features, barely discernible in daybreak's shadows. His eyes met hers, but there was a wariness there she thought she'd glimpsed before.

"Have you made your decision?" she asked baldly.

His gaze flared with surprise and then that wariness again, before he pulled the emotionless mask she'd come to hate into place.

"Do we need to talk about this now?"

"I think we do." She pulled out of his arms and sat up.

He followed suit, increasing the distance between them in the bed. It was only inches, but it felt like a great chasm.

"I do not think there can be any question that our test of sexual compatibility has been a success, can there?" he asked, his tone stilted unlike anything she'd heard from him before.

She couldn't think about the oddness of his delivery. Not when the words were so painful to hear. "Is that all the last weeks have been? A test?"

She jumped out of the bed, searching for her robe. Needing the protection of a layer of clothing between them, she yanked it on and tied the belt with jerky movements.

"No, *più amato*. That is not what I meant." He was out of bed, too, but he stood there naked in the predawn light.

He'd called her that before, on rare occasions, and only when their lovemaking was particularly intense. Another time she would ask what it meant, but right now her heart was threatening to shatter.

"How do I believe you?" she demanded, pain bleeding into her voice. "We have amazing sex, but that's all you let us have. We don't spend any time together."

"We are together every day."

She refused to believe in the desperation her heart wanted to tell her was in his tone. "With the children. Not alone."

"We are alone now."

"For sex."

"We are not having sex right now. That I know how to do. This…" He gestured between them. "*Us*. Talking about feelings. I do not know how to do this."

"How can you say that? You're an adult, a brilliant man. You're fluent in two languages."

"But not the language of emotions."

"If you felt them you could talk about them." Tears choked her throat and she went to turn away.

She needed a shower. Something. Anything away from him.

"No!" The word was loud, filled with power and with anguish.

She turned back to him.

"When would I have learned?" he demanded, fury and pain right there for her to see.

"What do you mean? You don't *learn* to love. You just feel it. And you can't teach someone to love you."

If she could have, she would have. Because not having his love when hers all but consumed her hurt more than any other rejection in her life or even all of them combined.

"You once said we are opposites," Enzu replied, with a desperation she could not deny this time.

But neither did she understand it. "Yes."

"I am a tycoon in business."

"And I'm a low-level employee for your company," she

said, unsure where he was going but unable to deny the entreaty in his blue gaze. "Our financial inequality certainly brought us together."

He frowned. "You don't like that."

"I hate it."

"Has it occurred to you that there is very little a billionaire might need he could not buy for himself?"

She'd only finished her Christmas shopping for him the day before. She was well aware of that fact. "Yes," she said with blatant sarcasm. "I do know."

"So you should realize what a gift it is for you to give me someone on whom to spend that money."

Seriously? That was his argument? "You have Franca and Angilu now."

"And you will guide me in how best to use my fortune to make their lives the best they can be."

Was he saying he *had* made his choice?

"It has been my delight to introduce you to the pleasures of the flesh," Vincenzo offered. "Your innocence is another gift my money could not buy."

"I don't understand where you are going with this."

"Indulge me, please."

She couldn't deny him. "Okay."

"You are very impulsive."

"And you're so controlled sometimes I think you could be a robot."

He winced. "With everyone and everything but you. *You make me lose control.*"

"And that's significant?"

"Very much so."

"I love you," she said, realizing that maybe he needed the words as much as she did. She'd said them before, but she felt the need to repeat them now.

"There is where we are most dissimilar."

"Because you don't love me?" she asked, agony exploding inside her.

"Because you are driven by emotion. You understand it. You are conversant in it. Tell me, what do you believe drives me?"

"Success." But that wasn't the whole truth. "Your desire to take care of your family."

"Yes, and in those things I am fluent."

"I know."

"But tell me, *amore,* who in my life has loved me? Who has allowed me to love them?"

She opened her mouth to say the children, but stopped herself. He wasn't talking about right now. He was talking about for his whole life up until now.

"You loved Pinu." She knew he had. "You love your parents. You took care of them. You still do."

"Pinu did not want my protection or affection. Neither do my parents."

"I think you're wrong. I think Pinu was thankful for your love even if you never told him in words. And he loved you, too. He named your nephew after you."

"You really believe that?" The vulnerability in her billionaire's expression was hard to see.

"I do."

"You are certain you love me? It is not just sex? Or the knowledge I can make things easier for Toby?"

She didn't take offence at Vincenzo's words. She couldn't. He *wasn't* fluent in the language of emotion. In fact he was as inept as a first-year language student in a foreign country.

"Yes, I love you. Very much."

"How do you *know?*"

She gave that question the full consideration it deserved. He needed her answer in a way she could never have foreseen.

"Because being with you makes me happier than when we are apart," she said finally. "Because I crave your presence in my life. Your texts make me smile, every single time I get one."

"I like being able to text you."

She nodded. "I can tell. I know I love you because the thought of living the rest of my life without you hurts more than anything else ever has."

Tension drained out of his body like air escaping a balloon and the most beautiful smile came over his face. *"T'amu."*

"What does that mean?" she asked, thinking she knew but needing to be absolutely sure.

"I love you."

She wanted to throw herself at him, but she asked, "Why in Sicilian?" Was he still trying to deny it in some way?

"Because, despite where I was born, my heart is Sicilian. If I am going to speak in the language of my heart it will come out in Sicilian first."

"Oh." Tears very different from the ones before burned her eyes. "What does *più amato* mean?"

"Best beloved. You are *it* for me, Audrey. Now and for all time." He swept her into his arms and kissed her breathless, then whispered against her hair. *"Ti vugghiu bini.* I love you *very* much."

"Me, too, Enzu." She pulled back, taking his face in her hands like he so often did with her. "I love you with everything in me. To me, you are life."

"And to me, you make life worth living. You make it real."

Their lovemaking after that was world-shattering, leaving their separate lives annihilated, nothing left but what they were together.

Christmas morning dawned bright and cold, a layer of snow turning the world around the mansion into a winter wonderland.

Franca could barely decide what she wanted more: to

open gifts or go outside and make snowmen with Toby. Toby, still very much a kid at heart in some ways, convinced the little girl that gifts were definitely more fun.

Vincenzo insisted the children open their gifts first. Audrey wanted to see each of their reactions, though she suspected the baby would enjoy the paper more than what was wrapped in it, so she didn't argue.

Though she was eager to see what Vincenzo thought of his homemade truffles.

Toby's shout of shocked delight after opening a gift from Vincenzo was loud enough to burst eardrums.

"What in the world...?" Audrey asked, unable to imagine this reaction to anything she and Vincenzo had picked out for her brother.

"It's MIT, Audrey." Toby jumped up and hugged the stuffing out of Vincenzo. "Thank you, Enzu. Thank you." He broke away from Vincenzo and waved the paper at Audrey. "Read it!"

With a confused smile, she took the single sheet and started reading. Emotion welled with each word she read.

Vincenzo had started a scholarship fund for bright students who got accepted into top schools but did not have the funds to attend despite their drive and ability. The first recipient would be Toby's best friend Danny.

Toby had got something even more, though. He'd got Vincenzo's solemn promise that no matter what happened between him and Audrey, Vincenzo would send Toby to MIT and whatever graduate school and PhD program he wanted to follow. All schooling and living expenses to be taken care of on two conditions: an above-average grade point and no drug use of any kind.

So like Vincenzo to put stipulations for Toby's benefit on the offer.

Audrey turned to Vincenzo, the paper dropping from her hand, her heart so full it could burst. "Thank you."

"I want you to know that if you wish to attend graduate school for your master's degree you will have my full support as well."

So much for thinking she could not be a loving mother with interests outside the home. Vincenzo had made a sea change in his thinking. But love could do that.

"Thank you," she said again. "Maybe someday."

He dropped to his knees in front of her. "Do not thank me. This is pure self-interest."

Both Audrey and Toby made identical sounds of disbelief.

Vincenzo just smiled. "Believe me. I have a question to ask you, Audrey, but I need your answer to have nothing to do with what is best for Toby."

"Oh." Audrey put her hand to her mouth, the emotion too big to contain.

Vincenzo presented her with a small wrapped box. She peeled the paper away with trembling fingers. Vincenzo helped her open the ring box—not because she needed it, but because it just felt right.

So, his big hands over hers, they opened the small velvet box to reveal a ring set beautifully with a cluster of chocolate diamonds.

"Your favorite," she choked out with a laugh.

"Like your eyes. Chocolate and filled with light."

"Oh, man. You are determined to make me cry."

"More desperate for you to say *yes,* and mean it for the *right* reasons. I love you, Audrey, with the whole of my Sicilian and American heart. Will you do me the utmost honor and marry me?"

"Yes. I love you, too, Enzu. So, so much! Oh, yes. Always, yes, Enzu!"

Then they were kissing, and hers weren't the only tears adding salty moisture to their lips.

Toby was whooping in the background and then so was Franca, and even the baby started his adorable giggling.

They were a family.

THEY WERE MARRIED on New Year's Eve, with Christmas décor still gracing the church, and Audrey carried a bouquet of crimson and white roses mixed with mistletoe and evergreen.

Toby said Vincenzo just wanted an excuse to kiss her whenever he wanted so the billionaire had supplied his own mistletoe. Vincenzo did not deny it, but he did manage to make Toby speechless when he asked the teen to sign the adult adoption papers that would make Toby a Tomasi.

"I'm not calling you Dad," Toby said, clearly overwhelmed with emotion.

"We are brothers, but you will be an official Tomasi and that is what matters. You belong to us."

Toby's grin split his face and he signed the papers with a flourish.

It was Audrey's turn to be speechless when a wedding guest who turned out to be a judge stepped forward to sign adoption papers for Franca and Angilu, officially making both Audrey and Vincenzo Tomasi their parents.

"How did you get the adoption through so fast?" Some legalities could only be expedited so much.

"I started proceedings the afternoon of your initial interview."

"What? How?"

"That non-disclosure agreement you signed?"

"Yes?"

"It may have included a power of attorney."

"You knew then?" she demanded.

He shrugged. "I had Gloria cancel the other candidates' interviews."

"You're a devious man, Enzu Tomasi, and in this case, I love you for it."

"I am so very glad to hear it, *più amato*. And you? You are my Christmas miracle."

She thought maybe that went both ways, but he was kissing her and she didn't get the chance to say so. She thought maybe he knew.

* * * * *

Available November 19, 2013

#3193 DEFIANT IN THE DESERT
Desert Men of Qurhah
by Sharon Kendrick

Middle Eastern diplomat Suleiman Abd al-Aziz has the *honor* of delivering the forbidden Sara Williams to her sheikh fiancé. But with his charge set on escaping marriage by seducing him and destroying her reputation, Suleiman's iron will is tested to the limit.

#3194 A HUNGER FOR THE FORBIDDEN
Sicily's Corretti Dynasty
by Maisey Yates

Alessia is a vision in white...as she flees the church. She's abandoned her fiancé, praying that his cousin Matteo Corretti will come after her, because there are two things Matteo doesn't know: Alessia is pregnant, and the child is his!

#3195 RUMORS ON THE RED CARPET
Scandal in the Spotlight
by Carole Mortimer

A dream holiday propels Thia Hammond from her quiet English life into the glittering world of Manhattan's scandalous elite—and the arms of internationally renowned mogul Lucien Steele! Now, she's about to learn about life and love in the fast lane....

#3196 NOT JUST THE BOSS'S PLAYTHING
by Caitlin Crews

From the moment Alicia Teller fell into Nikolai Korovin's arms, her ironclad control started to slip. After a night of pure, unadulterated passion, Alicia is horrified to walk into the boardroom on Monday morning to find a new but *very* familiar face!

#3197 THE PRINCE SHE NEVER KNEW
The Diomedi Heirs
by Kate Hewitt
Though the world believes in her high-profile romance with Prince Leo di Madina, Alyse Barras knows it's nothing but a calculated sham. But just as they begin to forge a tentative bond, a newspaper headline threatens to rip their fairy-tale ending apart.

#3198 THE CHANGE IN DI NAVARRA'S PLAN
by Lynn Raye Harris
Aspiring perfumer Holly Craig once naively gave in to the practiced charms of playboy Drago Di Navarra. Now the face of his next cosmetics campaign, Holly will prove she's become a more than worthy adversary for the intoxicating CEO....

#3199 HIS ULTIMATE PRIZE
by Maya Blake
Resisting ailing race-car driver Rafael de Cervantes is hard enough for physio Raven Blass without knowing *she* was responsible for the scars on his sculpted body. Will virgin Raven risk a night in Rafael's bed before he discovers the truth?

#3200 MORE THAN A CONVENIENT MARRIAGE?
by Dani Collins
Greek shipping magnate Gideon Vozaras appears to have it all, but behind the facade his perfect marriage is crumbling. Gideon can't afford the public scrutiny a divorce will bring, so he'll do everything in his power to keep what's his....
